DOCTOR WHO
G

D0285208

DOCTOR WHO
GALAXY FOUR

Based on the BBC television serial by William Emms by
arrangement with the British Broadcasting Corporation

WILLIAM EMMS

Number 104
in the
Doctor Who Library

TARGET

A TARGET BOOK

published by
the Paperback Division of
W. H. ALLEN & CO. PLC

A Target Book
Published in 1986
By the Paperback division of
W.H. Allen & Co. PLC
44 Hill Street, London, W1X 8LB

First published in Great Britain by
W. H. Allen & Co. PLC in 1985

Printed and bound in Great Britain by
Anchor Brendon Ltd, Tiptree, Essex

The BBC producer of *Galaxy Four* was
Verity Lambert, the director was Derek Martinus

ISBN 0 426 20202 3

CONTENTS

1

Four Hundred Dawns

The Doctor was puzzled. He had brought the TARDIS back into time and space, switched off the controls and turned on the external scanner. But as he moved the scanner from one angle to another he grew more uneasy. It wasn't that there was anything particularly wrong about the landscape he was viewing, at least not within his experience. In fact, it was quite appealing. But there was something wrong out there and he couldn't yet put his finger on exactly what it was.

The terrain wasn't exactly welcoming, he had to admit that. It was black, bearing a strong resemblance to tarmac. But numerous cracks had appeared in the surface and out of these trees and plant life had sprung in abundance. There were even flowers, though no evidence of how they were pollinated. He could see nothing even resembling a butterfly. Come to that, there was no sign of bird life either. He continued to stare intently at the screen.

Behind him Vicki was cutting Steven's hair. Her dark eyes moved from the job in hand to stare intently at the Doctor. 'Arrived, have we?'

The Doctor's attention remained on the screen. 'We have, my dear.'

Steven raised his head from the angle at which Vicki had tilted it. 'Good. Where?'

'Ah.' The Doctor examined the control panel. 'Somewhere in Galaxy Four. I don't know exactly where, I'm afraid. But . . . there's something not quite right about it.'

Steven stood up and he and Vicki crossed the console room to join the Doctor in staring at the screen. Neither was overly impressed. Vicki did not care for the black surface, though Steven did find a redeeming feature in the plants. He tousled his fair hair where Vicki had last been clipping and looked more closely. There was something distinctly odd about the scene, something missing. He felt uneasy. Like the Doctor, he could see no sign of animal life, but there was something else. After all, life could be underground, or even concealed somewhere in the greenery. So what was it?

'Could you put the sound on, please, Doctor?'

The Doctor checked his instruments and made an adjustment. 'It *is* on. Full now.'

They all listened intently and heard not a sound. The silence was quite overpowering. They could almost feel it. There was no sound whatsoever, not even of wind. All the trio could hear was their own breathing; all they could feel was the beating of their hearts.

'Weird,' whispered Vicki.

But the Doctor was again surveying his instruments. Everything was in satisfactory working order.

He stood back and sighed: 'Atmospheric pressure, temperature, oxygen content, radiation, all satisfactory.' He looked again at the scanner. 'I wonder if it's possible to have a planet so obviously conducive to life, yet . . . without any?'

'Well, I've finished chopping Steven's hair. Can we go out and see?'

The Doctor shrugged. 'I don't see why not. There's just a chance that we might get some peace.'

'For a change,' Steven added dryly. 'Perhaps there's even a river or a lake. Fancy a swim, Doctor?'

'Young man, this is a scientific expedition,' the Doctor replied tartly. 'It pays always to be cautious.'

'There's a limit to –' Steven broke off as something banged against the side of the TARDIS.

They looked at each other, startled, and there was yet another bump. The Doctor raised his hand for silence. Whatever it was continued to keep knocking against the TARDIS, proceeding along one side, then another, obviously investigating the machine. And now they could hear something else: a curious chittering and jingling sound, obviously emanating from the intruder.

'What is it?' Vicki whispered.

'Something mechanical,' the Doctor answered. 'A robot of some sort.'

'But why the knocking?' Steven wondered.

'I would guess that it's blind and has to proceed by touch,' the Doctor said.

The knocking ceased, the intruder having completed its circuit of the TARDIS. It fell silent and they heard it moving away.

9

'Look,' Vicki said, pointing at the screen.

They followed her gaze and saw their visitor. It was a short, round structure made of some metallic substance. It could not have stood much more than four feet in height. The body consisted of a round base, a rather larger main body and a smaller shoulder section. The facial section was a grill, surmounted by a skull-like cap from which antennae protruded. The grill contained what looked very much like a gun. It came to a halt some ten metres away and faced the TARDIS again. A series of coloured lights started flashing in its head and it emitted a soft, high note.

The Doctor was fascinated. He noted too that around the base were a number of pear-shaped instruments which he took to be sensors.

'It looks to me as though it's sending a message,' Steven said.

The Doctor nodded. 'To its controllers, whoever they are.'

Steven grimaced. 'Or *whatever* they are.'

The robot was on the move again. It turned and began to trundle away. Vicki was still staring at it. 'Look how it moves,' she said. 'It's got a sort of "chumbley" movement.'

Steven stared at her in disbelief. '*Chumbley*?'

'Yes. Can't you see?' Her attractive face weakened as she nearly lost conviction. 'All sort of . . . chumbley.'

'Well, he's gone now,' the Doctor said. But he was thinking how wrong he had been in deciding there was no life on the planet. Not only was there life, but highly intelligent life at that. It took considerable technical skill and knowledge to bring into being a robot such as they had been watching. The question was: what sort of intelligence? He had encountered many varieties of intelligent life forms and not all of them had been friendly. Well, there was only one way to find out.

'We'll have the doors open,' he said.

Steven was recalling the Doctor's previous words of caution. 'Wouldn't it be better to wait for a while? Those things might be dangerous.'

But the Doctor ignored him. He pressed the control button and the door swung open. Picking up his stick, he made for the open air, a strange but brave sight in his battered trousers and frock coat, cravat fluttering about his neck, and his white hair not as tidy as it might have been. Vicki and Steven exchanged a slightly worried glance, then followed. Once outside, the Doctor breathed in deeply and with enjoyment. 'Delightful. Just the right oxygen content.'

'And the flowers smell lovely,' Vicki said.

Steven, however, was shielding his eyes and looking into the sky. 'I see we've got three suns. I wonder which one we revolve around?'

The Doctor finished locking the door of the TARDIS. 'It's quite possible that they revolve around us.' He straightened and pocketed the key, glanced at Vicki who was examining the flowers, then at the terrain surrounding them. It reminded him of a past experience. 'The silence is just like it was on the planet Xeros.'

Vicki turned from examining the flowers. 'We haven't jumped a time-track again, have we?'

11

'No, no, my child. Not this time.' He tilted his head to the side. 'But I don't like the silence. Not at all.'

Vicki gasped. 'Doctor!'

The Doctor and Steven looked at her, then followed her pointing finger. A Chumbley had appeared from behind the TARDIS and was obviously sensing them. Lights were flashing on the grill of this one as well. But what made it decidedly ominous was that its gun was pointed directly at them.

'Keep still,' the Doctor said. 'Don't do anything to alarm it.'

He moved cautiously nearer the machine, examining it carefully. Ignoring his admonition, Steven also moved, but sideways, hoping to be able to do some damage once out of range of the gun.

For lack of anything more inspiring to do, the Doctor addressed the machine: 'We wish you no harm. We come in peace.'

The robot remained stationary and silent.

'I don't think it can speak,' Vicki said.

But the Doctor was still observing and noting that beneath the head-grill was what looked very much to be a speaker. It had the necessary mesh covering which gave it every evidence of being a sound-box. Why, then, did it remain silent?

It didn't, however, remain silent for long. From it suddenly came a rapid chittering sound, like that of a tape being run backwards at speed. Equally as suddenly it stopped. The Doctor was fascinated. He had no idea what it was trying to say, or even if it was directed at them. It could just as well be transmitting a message back to its unknown controller. He remained still.

12

But Steven did not. Slowly he crouched to pick up a lump of black rock. What he had not calculated upon was the slight sound he made in doing so. In a flash the Chumbley backed a little and trained its gun on him.

The Doctor was exasperated. 'You idiot!'

'I was only trying to –'

'Yes, yes, very noble of you,' the Doctor cut in. 'Now that thing is on its guard and we could be in deep trouble.' He paused a moment. 'Interesting, though. Did you notice that it wasn't aware of what you were doing until you made a noise?'

Steven nodded. 'So it's blind.'

'But it can hear,' Vicki said.

'And very accurately at that,' the Doctor added. 'It might also be locating us by heat waves, or something of the sort.'

Again came the chittering sound and the Chumbley moved forward, heading for the Doctor. It reached him and nudged him. The Doctor stepped back. It did the same again, pushing him back yet another step. Then it turned and headed for Vicki and Steven, obviously intent on giving them the same treatment.

'It's trying to get us to go somewhere,' Vicki said.

'Indeed,' the Doctor agreed. 'But stand still. Don't let it move you.'

The Chumbley nudged against them both in turn and each stepped back into place as soon as the opportunity offered. It would have been an amusing sight were it not for the gun constantly covering them.

Finally the Chumbley backed away and remained still for a moment, clearly receiving a message. Then

13

it chittered briefly to itself and rotated its gun until it pointed at some vegetation. The three looked on with some trepidation as a brilliant white ray leapt out, accompanied by a piercingly high shriek. It swept across the greenery and turned all into flame. Then the ray cut off and the gun turned back to them.

'As neat a threat as I ever saw,' the Doctor said. 'We'd better do what the thing wants.'

They grouped together and set off across the dark landscape in the direction the Chumbley had indicated. The Chumbley came jinking after them. Then it scooted up to the front, then to the side, then back behind them, for all the world like a destroyer herding a convoy into harbour. It occurred to the Doctor that as well as guiding them, it seemed almost to be guarding them. He glanced again about him, but could still see no movement. Perhaps the thing was programmed to a certain pattern of behaviour and had no alternative but to behave as it did.

Drahvins One and Two watched the group approach the ledge on which they had hidden themselves. They were women. They had long, blonde hair and would have been considered extremely attractive by any man were it not for the total lack of warmth in their faces which were straight and set, reflecting no emotion whatsoever. Both wore the same dark, high-necked uniform dress and each carried a gun, rather like a twentieth-century Earth machine-gun, except that what came from the barrel could not possibly be bullets. Where the man-made variety carried a bullet clip these had a power pack. The Drahvins held them confidently. They well knew how to use them.

As the sound of the Chumbley grew louder Drahvin Two set down her gun and grasped one side of a sheet of metallic mesh which lay at her feet. Her companion took the other side and they waited, stony-faced, as the party came into view beneath them, the Doctor leading, Vicki and Steven behind him, and the Chumbley following up.

The Drahvins moved to the edge, awaited the right moment, then hurled the mesh down on the Chumbley. As soon as the mesh enveloped it the machine came to an abrupt halt and fell silent. Two immediately picked up her gun and ran down the bank toward the Doctor. One remained on guard, also now once again armed.

The Doctor came to a halt and looked cautiously at the beautiful woman approaching. It seemed to him that there was something of a surplus of weapons on this planet. He did not greatly care for that. Nor was he much taken with the way they always seemed to be pointed at him, as this one was. It might well have a beautiful woman at the end of it, but her eyes looked cold and intense.

'Who is she?' Vicki wondered.

'I've no idea,' Steven said. 'But she's a lovely surprise.'

Two lowered her gun slightly. 'We are the Drahvin.'

'And what might the Drahvin be?' asked the Doctor.

'We are from the planet Drahva in Galaxy Four.'

The Doctor nodded. He was familiar with that part of the universe, though not the exact planet. 'And what do you want of us?'

'We came to rescue you.' She nodded in the direction of the immobilised Chumbley. 'They are our enemies.'

'Why?' Steven wanted to know.

'Maaga will tell you.'

'Maaga?'

'Our leader.'

'Why don't you tell us?' said the Doctor. 'That would seem to be the quickest way.'

Her eyes chilled him. 'Our mission was to rescue you. We have done that. We have no other instructions but to take you to Maaga. If you stay here more machines will come and you will be captured and taken to the Rills.'

The Doctor watched as One approached and stood beside her companion. He noted their similar clothing and the same absence of expression. There was something odd about these two. They weren't physical clones, that was true, but he wondered if in some way they might be mental ones. It was not beyond the bounds of possibility. Something had to explain their lack of emotion.

'Are the Rills the people who control these machines?'

'They are not people,' Two answered.

'They are things,' One added.

'They crawl.'

'They murder.'

Vicki jumped. 'Murder?'

'They have already killed one of us.'

The Doctor nodded in agreement. 'All right, we'll go and talk to Maaga.'

16

Vicki stepped forward and grabbed his arm, pointing into the distance. 'Look.'

In the distance were four Chumblies. They were heading toward them, their visors flickering with colour and their wheels bubbling over obstacles as though they did not exist. Their direction was clear and their intent easily guessed. Yet they did not seem to Vicki as menacing as the two women standing before her. Something about them did not ring true. There was a vacancy about them she could not quite put her finger on.

But the two were busy, trying to retrieve the mesh from the Chumbley. Yet no matter how they pulled it would not move. The Chumbley stood quite still, not a flicker of life in it, but the mesh would not come free, despite their frantic efforts.

'It's caught somewhere,' One gasped.

'Or the robot is magnetised to make sure you can't get it off,' the Doctor observed.

'But we must. We were instructed not to lose it.'

Steven watched the Chumblies advancing like mechanised cavalry. 'Were you instructed to be killed as well? They're pretty close.

Two looked over her shoulder. 'We must go. Come with us.'

The Doctor shrugged at his young friends and they set off after the Drahvins, Two waving her gun at them to encourage speed.

Behind them, the pursuers reached the trapped Chumbley and encircled it. One of them stood before it, chittered a while, then extended a clawed arm, grasped the mesh and effortlessly pulled it clear.

17

Immediately it came to life, visor flashing, turned and set off with its comrades after the Doctor and his party.

They had a surprising turn of speed and the party had to run to stay ahead of them, the Doctor soon wishing that he had found a younger body to inhabit. There was not a lot to be said for this one. In no time at all his hearts were hammering, his lungs labouring like a pair of ancient bellows and his limbs moving only with the greatest of reluctance. Steven turned back and put an arm about him to help him, but his assistance did little to improve things. This was an old body and there was nothing to be done about it, despite the hectoring calls from the two Drahvins for more haste.

He was about to give up entirely when Steven gasped, 'There it is, Doctor.'

The Doctor looked up and there before him was the Drahvin spaceship. It was some fifty metres in length, observation ports lining its side, a badly damaged aerial protruding from the top. There were serious burns in its sides and several patched holes. It had obviously been in a battle and taken a lot of punishment. But at least it offered sanctuary, for which the Doctor would be deeply grateful. With one huge last effort he forced himself onward until they reached the ship's entry. It slid open and they piled inside, all out of breath.

'Close external door,' One snapped.

A voice came from a speaker above them. 'Close external door.'

It slid shut and Vicki leaned exhausted against the

observation panel to see the Chumblies come to a halt just outside. She could see their visors flashing and knew that they were reporting back, though she could hear nothing as yet. She turned away. 'Are you all right, Doctor?'

The Doctor emptied his lungs, then inhaled deeply. 'I think so. I'm just not very good at physical exercise these days. This body's wearing out.'

'Oh, it should last a while yet,' Steven said.

'God bless you for those words of comfort.'

'You're welcome.'

The Doctor turned to the Drahvins: 'What now?'

'We shall go inside,' Two said. 'Follow me.'

She pressed her hand against a light in the bulkhead and another door slid open. She led the way into the adjoining compartment. This too, the Doctor noticed, was somewhat battered. Clearly, some attempt had been made to clear up the damage, but holed metal needs tools and he surmised that these were in short supply. The table to the side had one leg on chocks and the chairs looked none too sure of themselves. The shelving listed. A desk had been torn away from the deck and now stood forlornly to the bulkhead. Originally spartan, the compartment now looked utterly cheerless, no effort ever having been made to brighten it in the first place.

'Warm and cosy,' he muttered to himself. 'A nice place to die.'

'Biggish, isn't it?' Steven said, looking about him.

'And more than a little backward, by the look of it,' the Doctor replied. 'The machinery I can see looks fairly primitive.'

19

'It got them through space,' Vicki said.

The Doctor nodded. 'Just.'

Another Drahvin entered. She too wore the same uniform as the others. She too was blonde. She too had the same absence of expression. Steven was beginning to think that they looked like mobile dolls. For all he knew, that was precisely what they were. Whatever the truth of it, he was beginning to dislike attractive women who showed no sign of feeling.

'Silence. Maaga is coming,' the third one said.

Maaga stepped into the room. She also was blonde, but something about her was different. Her face was lively and her eyes bright. She glanced briefly at the trio, then addressed Drahvin Two: 'Report.'

Drahvin Two stood rigidly at attention, as did her companion. 'Mission accomplished. We have brought the prisoners.'

'Prisoners?' Vicki wondered aloud.

But Maaga was not yet interested in her. 'And the mesh sheet?'

'It stopped the machine.'

'Good.'

Now One spoke, though the Doctor was interested to note that she now showed a trace of emotion – that of fear. 'We could not get the mesh back again. It became affixed to the machine.'

Maaga was clearly angry. The Doctor felt he should intervene in the interests of fair play. 'I think you'll find it was magnetised,' he said.

Maaga glanced briefly at him, then returned to her two subordinates. 'I will deal with you both later. Sit.'

They crossed to the chairs and did so, though they

sat to attention, obviously in awe of their leader. Their faces lapsed into the normal lack of expression.

Maaga turned back to the Doctor. 'I'm sorry to have kept you waiting, but I had to hear the report first. Please sit down.'

The Doctor grunted his thanks and did so. He waited expectantly for her to speak.

'We are at war, you see,' she said.

Now the Doctor really was interested. 'War? With whom?'

'The Rills and their machines. It's a fight to the death. One of us has to be obliterated.'

'As bad as that?' the Doctor asked.

'Very bad indeed. So bad that it is conceivable you too will be obliterated.'

Vicki was angry. She had no liking at all either for the ship or its inhabitants. Nor did she greatly care for what seemed to be a threat. Who did this woman think she was? 'Who's going to do that: you or the Rills?'

Maaga was unmoved by her anger. 'When a planet disintegrates nothing survives.'

The Doctor was suddenly alert. 'Disintegrates? I take it you mean *this* planet?'

'Correct. It is in its last moments of life. Soon it will explode, taking all life forms with it. If my claculations are correct – and they usually are – that will happen in fourteen dawns' time.'

Steven was not only alarmed. He was suspicious. 'How can you be so certain?'

'You don't have to take my word for it. The Rills contacted us by radio and confirmed my figures. That is why they are repairing their spaceship – so that they can escape.' A look of determination came onto her face. 'And that is why we must capture it from them.'

Steven raised an eyebrow at Vicki. He was far from used to women having such an attitude. He preferred the old-fashioned type, gentle, loving, fond of homely things. The warlike variety did not win him over at all.

'Our ship is powerless,' Maaga continued. 'We were innocently seeking a planet we could colonise when the Rills appeared and attacked us. My crew fought well, but the Rills' armament was superior to ours. We damaged them all right and they had to come down, as we did. But I think their problems are less serious than ours, which is why we want their ship.'

'And how will you get it?' the Doctor asked.

'We shall fight our way in and take over.'

'And the Rills?'

'They are of no importance.'

The Doctor nodded. He could see that the Drahvins had little respect for life. But the question uppermost in his mind was: would they respect that of Vicki, Steven and himself? The woman before him gave little evidence of such an inclination. Nor did her subordinates, sitting like graven images at the table. He wondered briefly why he always managed to materialise in a trouble spot, then returned his attention to Maaga. 'Have you travelled far?'

'We come from Drahva. But the vegetation is dying there. Our planet is cooling, so we have to find another which is habitable. There is not a lot of time left.'

22

'Where are your men?' Steven asked. 'Or are they back at home feeding the swans?'

She looked at him in puzzlement. 'Men?'

'Males,' the Doctor prompted. 'The counterpart of the female species.'

Her face cleared. 'Ah, those. We have a small number of them, but no more than is necessary for our purpose. The rest were killed. They consumed valuable food and served no particular purpose. After all, why keep parasites? No civilization can go on doing that, especially when its planet is dying.' She gestured disdainfully in the direction of her crew. 'And these are not what you would call . . . human. They are cultivated in test tubes as and when called for. We have very good scientists.'

'All female, of course,' Vicki said, noting that the crew still sat rigid and motionless despite the condescension of Maaga's words.

'Naturally,' Maaga said. 'I, by the way, am a normal life form. My crew are mere products and inferior at that.' She surveyed them with no look of fondness in her eyes. 'They are grown for a purpose and are capable of nothing more.'

'And what is the purpose?' the Doctor asked.

'To serve. To fight. To kill.'

'What an interesting place Drahva must be.' He pondered a moment. 'You're quite sure the Rills attacked you?'

Maaga sighed. 'We were in space above this planet when we saw a ship such as we had never seen before. We didn't know it, but it was the Rills' ship. It fired on us and we were brought down. But before we did

23

we succeeded in firing back so that their ship crashed as well. They managed to kill one of my soldiers.'

Steven remembered what the two Drahvins had told him at the outset. 'What do they look like, these Rills?'

'Disgusting,' Maaga said.

'That's no description – no description at all.'

'It's all I will say.'

'But now I begin to understand,' the Doctor murmured.

'So do I,' Steven said. 'This planet is going to explode and they're managing to repair their ship in time. You haven't, so you want theirs.'

'We do not wish to be here when this planet ceases to exist. Do you?'

Before Steven could reply, Drahvin Three, who had been on watch at an observation window, turned and called, 'Machine approaching.'

'To your stations,' Maaga snapped, crossing to the window. The other did the same, at another window. They saw one of the Rills' machines chumbling across the landscape toward them, visor flashing and gun at the ready. Vicki thought again that she found them most attractive little machines. There was something almost human about them, though she knew such a thing was almost certainly impossible. A machine was a machine was a machine was a machine and that was the end of it. Even so . . . She thought it a pity that they would very likely turn out to be the enemy, particularly since that would make the Drahvins their allies. The situation was not overly full of promise.

Maaga and her soldiers had now crossed to

protrusions from the bulkhead and were pressing numerous buttons. Canopies swung away, revealing two-grip guns and aiming ports. The guns looked as though they could do their job effectively, as did the Drahvins manning them.

Maaga peered through her aiming port, her expression one of determination. 'Load,' she commanded.

Each pressed another button and quiet red lights glowed forward of the grips.

'Prepare to fire. Switch off the outside radio.'

Drahvin Two knocked up a switch.

'Why do that?' the Doctor asked.

'They send the machines to tell us lies,' Maaga said tightly. 'We do not want to hear them.'

'Possibly not, but we'd like to.'

But Maaga ignored him. The Chumbley was stationary now and the Doctor could see that it was speaking its message. It seemed a pity he couldn't hear it. There was something odd about the Rills trying to contact the Drahvins and receiving nothing but animosity in return. But then, he would put nothing past the hard-faced Maaga and her mindless minions.

'*Fire!*' Maaga snapped.

There was a harsh hissing sound and rays leapt out from the guns at the Chumbley. The machine was enveloped in smoke and glowed bright red from the attack. But its visor was covered now and it remained where it was. Still the rays stabbed at it as the Drahvins triggered their weapons again and again, and still the Chumbley remained. It looked to the Doctor very much as though the outer plating was protective, possibly even absorbing the energy hurled at it and using it, which would make the attack totally futile.

'Cease fire,' Maaga snapped and the rays vanished.

The smoke cleared from the Chumbley and they could see that it was still intact. It chittered briefly to itself and the shield vanished from its visor. Its lights still flickered busily away. Maaga took careful aim and her ray shot out at the visor. But it was an exercise in pointlessness. The visor was covered again before the ray was halfway there. Maaga grunted in exasperation. 'Damn them.'

But the Doctor was impressed. Any intelligence which could produce a machine capable of reacting faster than a laser beam aimed at it had to be of a high order, even if it was evil and disgusting. He would definitely like to meet the Rills.

The Chumbley chittered briefly, its visor once again open, received instructions, turned and moved away. It vanished over a hill, looking totally unconcerned about what had happened to it, bent upon tending to its own affairs.

'Well, you didn't do him much damage, did you?' Steven commented.

'My only intention was to drive it off,' Maaga said coldly. 'We have succeeded.' She turned to her soldiers. 'Disarm and return to your places.'

They promptly obeyed, switching everything off, re-covering the guns and crossing to sit again, all with immaculate timing, as though they themselves were machines guided by a centralised computer.

'Zombies,' Vicki muttered to herself.

'You haven't destroyed a single one of those

machines yet, have you?' the Doctor said.

Maaga was closing down her own gun. 'We will.'

'I think you underestimate the Rills. And why, I wonder, should they warn you that this planet is about to die?'

'To tempt us to their ship so that they could kill us.'

'But they did offer to help you,' Steven said.

'That is what they claimed.'

'But they might have been telling the truth,' Vicki insisted. 'They might have meant it.'

'Yes, and it might all have been lies too,' the Doctor said thoughtfully.

Maaga nodded. 'That is precisely what I have been saying.'

The Doctor grew testy. 'I mean that you could all be wrong and this planet might last for another billion years.'

'We do not make mistakes like that.'

'Really? Then yours is a very rare species indeed.' The Doctor warmed to his theme. 'In all my travels I've never come across anyone or anything that wasn't capable of error. Even *I* have been known to make the odd mistake. And, if I might say so, you don't look like any particular sort of genius to me. You can't even work out how to stop one of those robots. You put up a very fancy display, blazing away like that, but what did it amount to in the end? Nothing.' He waved absently in the direction of the rigid Drahvins. 'And you surround yourself with poor half-wits like these. No, no, no, it won't do at all. Your performance does not match up to your high opinion of yourself. You're as bad as that fellow Plato I once ran into. I

27

never did manage to get it across to him that you cannot build a lasting civilisation upon slavery, no matter how benign the masters. The old question rears its ugly head: how do you explain to a fool that he's a fool?' He checked his temper as best he could. 'You'd better let me run my own tests for you.'

Maaga was offended by his outburst. 'And what makes you think you can do that?'

'I'm a scientist, woman. I know about these things.'

She thought a moment, then nodded. 'Very well.'

'Then we'll have to go back to the TARDIS. If you'll excuse us . . .' He moved toward the door, indicating that Vicki and Steven should join him.

'No,' Maaga said. 'You cannot all go.'

'Oh? Why not?' the Doctor asked.

Vicki felt her suspicions confirmed. 'We *are* prisoners, aren't we?'

'Of course not. But if you should encounter the machines . . .'

'What of it?' Steven said.

'We could not guarantee to rescue you again.'

The Doctor waved her away. 'Oh, you worry too much.'

'I would feel easier if one of you remained here,' Maaga said firmly.

It was a state of deadlock, the familiar Mexican stand-off. Doubt and suspicion hung heavy in the air. The Doctor did not want his group split up, but equally he could see no other way out. Maaga had the upper hand and she knew it. It showed in her face. There was too much arrogance about the woman, he decided. He would have to try and do something about that.

'I'll stay,' Vicki said in a tight voice, seeing no other way out of the impasse.

The Doctor was about to protest, but she cut across him. 'You'll need Steven if you run into the Chumblies.'

The Doctor had to concede. 'Very well. We'll be as quick as we can. Come along, young man.'

Maaga gestured to Two. She got up and opened the door and exit lock for them and the Doctor hastened out. Steven paused before following him and gave Vicki a reassuring smile. 'I promise we won't get lost.'

'Please don't,' Vicki said in a small voice.

Steven went out and she was left alone with the Drahvins. The prospect of no company but theirs for a time did nothing to cheer her. Ah well, there was nothing for it but to wait in hope.

The Doctor and Steven moved away from the battered ship. They went cautiously, wary of attack, but of the two Steven was the more cautious, the Doctor having lost himself again in a pool of thought. He was brooding upon the fourteen dawns of life left for the planet. The trouble was that he did not know what technology either the Drahvins or the Rills had used to determine the planet's remaining life-span. It could be quite primitive in the case of the former, but the latter had shown themselves capable of producing highly sophisticated robots, so he was inclined to believe them. Unless, as Maaga had said, they were simply trying to lead the Drahvins into a trap. There were too many ifs about the whole project for his liking and there was only one way to resolve them. He stepped up his pace as they went toward the top of the rise leading to the TARDIS.

But Steven, a little ahead of him, waved for him to stop as he peered over. The Doctor crouched and joined him.

'Company,' Steven said briefly.

There, below them, stood the TARDIS, a battered old police telephone box to all intents and purposes and looking very much out of place in its surroundings. Also within their field of vision were two Chumblies standing before the door. One was making obvious attempts to get in, a clawed arm raking at the lock. But it made no impression whatsoever, rake as it might. The Doctor smiled to himself. They would have to do a lot better than that.

Finally the first one desisted and turned away, to be replaced by the other. This one had more telling equipment. Jamming itself against the door it extended what looked to the observers very much like a drill.

It was a drill. Its grinding scream reached them easily as yet another attack was made on the lock. The pressure was so great that showers of sparks flew out and the Chumbley itself tottered from side to side in its efforts to hold the drill in place. From behind and above it looked like a round-bottomed old lady pottering about her domestic duties, the Doctor thought. But its intention was much more serious.

'Can they get in?' Steven asked worriedly.

'I shouldn't think so.'

'Don't you know?'

The Doctor nodded. 'Pretty well. They'd have to be

30

extremely advanced to break my force barrier.'

Steven watched the Chumbley make another attempt. 'How do you know they aren't?'

But the Doctor didn't answer. He smiled interestedly down on the scene. A challenge always pleased him and here were the Rills and their robots challenging his knowledge of technology. Well, good luck to them. He had every confidence in himself.

Vicki was seated alone in the Drahvin living quarters. She felt unhappy, primarily about the solitude, but also about her conviction that Maaga meant them no good. She had been fed some form of tablet food and given a sickly-sweet drink to quench her thirst, but what she wanted most of all was her liberty. The bulkheads of this dingy ship dripped fear and threat and she was sure they did so with good reason.

It was odd that the only emotion the Drahvin minions had revealed was that of fear – and that only of Maaga. The Chumblies had frightened them not at all in either of their encounters, but Maaga was an altogether different proposition. She wondered if they were test-tube bred in such a way that the awe was born in them or if it was instilled after birth. If the latter was the case she felt sorry for them. It must have been a terrible upbringing.

Not that she was in a mood to spare much sympathy for them as she got to her feet and wandered aimlessly about the cabin. She was more concerned about the Doctor, Steven and herself. What had they got themselves into this time?

She stilled as she heard voices in the next compartment,

some quiet, one harsh and bullying. Then she crossed to the adjoining bulkhead and pressed her ear against it. The harsh voice she could hear was that of Maaga. Vicki pressed even closer.

'To lose the mesh was gross incompetence,' she heard Maaga snarl. 'It was our only weapon against the machines. If we lose to the Rills it will be because of you. You want that, do you?' Her voice became sneering. 'You want to be captured by those creeping, revolting green monsters? You want their slimy claws about your necks?'

Vicki could hear the Drahvins moaning in a terror induced solely by their leader.

'You fools! You fools!' she heard. 'You will all be punished when I have time to attend to it.'

Again came the moaning and a horrified Vicki shrank away into her icy loneliness.

The Chumbley was still drilling away at the lock of the TARDIS and achieving the same result: it had no effect whatsoever. The lock remained as it always had been, old, rusted and impervious. The Chumbley backed away, retracted the drill and seemed to stand a moment in contemplation. This, it would appear, was something quite beyond its experience, the enigma beyond the puzzle. But, not to be defeated too easily, it had one more try. Its gun came down and pointed at the lock. A moment later the light beam flashed out and locked in a blaze of flame on the keyhole. Some ten seconds later the Chumbley desisted and the smoke cleared. Another useless attempt. The TARDIS stood as it always had, in supreme indifference.

The Chumbley backed away and turned. The lights in its visor came to life and flickered busily as it communicated with its controller. Then they went out again. Both Chumblies made their way off into the distance, mission most decidedly not accomplished.

Once they were out of sight the Doctor and Steven scrambled their way down to the TARDIS. The Doctor immediately went to the lock and was well pleased. 'Look at that, my boy,' he said. 'Not a scratch. Not even a scorch-mark. I excelled myself with that force field, I really did.'

There were occasions when Steven found it difficult to distinguish between pride and conceit in the Doctor. He sighed, 'Are we going inside or not?'

The Doctor started. 'What? Oh, yes, yes, yes.' He took the key from his pocket and opened the TARDIS door. 'Good job you're here to remind me what I'm supposed to be doing, eh?'

'You're so right,' Steven said, following him in.

Once they were inside, the doors closed behind them. The Doctor crossed to the control panel and began to press a button here and a button there, his fingers seeming to know more about what they were doing than he did himself. Steven watched as, that series of operations completed, he took to adjusting dials one after another. Finally he grunted and straightened up. He flicked a switch and the astral map came to glowing life on the screen above the panel.

'That's the stuff,' the Doctor muttered, eyeing the dots on the map, each one representing a planet in the sector in which they now found themselves. He made some more adjustments, then pressed another button. One of the dots became a pulsating glow of red. 'There we are, Steven, now we know our exact whereabouts.'

'Do we?'

'Well, I do. That'll suffice for the moment. Now . . .' He moved to the side and began to work over more buttons and dials, but thoughtfully this time, considering each move he was making. 'Let's see if we can work the oracle.'

Steven looked on in fascination. 'Don't you know?'

'Not always. This instrument takes time to adjust to new surroundings and we haven't been here long.'

'Long enough for me.'

But the Doctor was lost again in his instruments. He stared at the astral map. Nothing happened. He clicked his tongue in annoyance. 'What a time to choose to become temperamental!'

'No luck?' Steven asked.

'All is not yet lost.' He returned to his work, glancing repeatedly at the screen, then slowly turned one last dial, his face tense, his eyes narrowed. And there on the screen appeared two lines of numbers and symbols Steven had never seen before.

'That's it,' the Doctor said in satisfaction. He slid open a drawer and withdrew a heavy book which he set down on the panel. Constantly glancing at the screen he leafed this way and that through the pages. 'Now we'll find out just what is happening.'

Steven could sense his concentration and said nothing. He felt like a prisoner in court as he awaited the verdict, always assuming there was one on the way. An erratic man was the Doctor and as likely to go one way as another. He contained himself until the Doctor looked up.

'Well, Doctor?' he said.

The Doctor met his eyes, but his thoughts were obviously elsewhere. 'The Rills were right. This planet is doomed.'

'Then we'd better get off it, hadn't we?'

'That would seem the most sensible course. But do you think the Drahvins will let us?'

Steven shrugged. 'What are we to them?'

'A possible means of escape,' the Doctor said. 'Surely you saw their killer instinct. They want our help to wipe out the Rills, so that they can take their ship and clear off out of it.'

'Why haven't they had a shot at the TARDIS, then?'

'That's just it. They've got their priorities wrong. Kill first, escape afterwards.' He gave a smile in which there was no humour. 'Odd, isn't it? Such attractive life forms, yet with that stream of evil running through them.'

'You can't be sure of that.' Steven didn't know why he should appear to be defending the Drahvins other than that he was reluctant to believe such beauty walking hand in hand with the figure of death.

'Possibly not,' the Doctor said crisply. 'But I can give you odds of nine to four. Why d'you think they kept Vicki back: concern for her health?'

'It's the logical thing to do. How were they to know we wouldn't come back to the TARDIS and simply take off?'

35

'That is something we'd be well advised to do. And quickly, at that.'

'We've got fourteen dawns.'

The Doctor looked at him quizzically. 'No, we haven't. We've got two. Tomorrow is the last day this planet will see.'

2

Trap of Steel

The suns spun leisurely through space above the planet. Thus it always had been and thus it would stay, an observer would have thought. But when the planet went they too would go. First would come a throbbing pulsation through the emptiness as the planet began to expand outward, its surface beginning to split asunder and lava to spit and pour outward. Then an unholy white light would dance this way and that across the surface and the last moment would come. The planet and its suns would go nova, a brief spot of light in eternal space and of no consequence in time. From then on they would be of no consequence in space either, mere boulders rolling their way through eternity.

The Doctor knew this as he watched the shock on Steven's face. He felt some sympathy for the lad. After all, strictly speaking this was not his field. He had been wrenched into it by unforeseeable circumstances and had borne up gamely whereas he, the Doctor, had learnt to adapt since time immemorial. Human life wasn't long enough, he thought, no sooner given than taken away, with insufficient time to learn what was necessary or do what had to be done. He dismissed the thought. There was nothing he could do about it. He wasn't God, simply something of a clown in his own eyes, trolling about through time and space seeking the final truth as he inhabited one body after another, and yet with the dull feeling that that final truth would remain forever beyond his reach.

This wouldn't do. 'We have to worry about Vicki,' he said quietly.

Steven shook off his numbness. 'That we must. And right away, at that.'

Fishing in his pocket for the key, the Doctor headed for the door. But Steven stopped him. 'Hang on, Doctor. Let's check first.'

He made for the scanner to view outside and straightaway saw a Chumbley heading toward them. 'Take a look at this,' he said.

The Doctor came up beside him to see what the scanner revealed. He saw the robot coming in across the black landscape, but was more interested in what it was carrying, a phial-shaped object about seventeen inches long and eight inches wide.

'What is it?' Steven wondered.

'I don't know.' The Doctor squinted at the picture. 'Whatever it is, I'd guess it isn't intended to improve the quality of our lives.'

'It's wasting our time.'

'We don't have any alternative but to stay, do we?'

'I suppose not.'

'Then try to be patient.'

The Chumbley moved right in until it bumped into

the TARDIS. It paused a moment, chuttering to itself, then leaned the phial against the door, released it and moved back a little. Again a brief pause and it turned about and moved off. Now the Doctor and Steven could see that it was trailing a wire from each of its two claws. This did not look in the least bit promising.

'What was that?' Steven asked.

The Doctor was pensive. 'I wish I knew. They haven't actually harmed us yet, but it's possible they're losing patience.'

'I don't like the look of those wires.'

'Nor do I. We'll have to try something.' He flicked on the outside speakers of the TARDIS and spoke into the microphone. 'You out there. Can you hear me?'

The Chumbley remained still.

'We come in peace. We come as friends. Please answer if you can hear me.'

Nothing happened. The utter stillness of the machine was unnerving, particularly since it still grasped the two wires which had to serve some purpose, not necessarily one in their favour.

'It can hear us all right,' the Doctor muttered. 'So why no answer? They contacted the Drahvins without any trouble.'

'Maybe they didn't like the way the Drahvins responded. After all, they –'

He was cut off by a tremendous explosion, the sound of which ripped through the TARDIS and tore at their eardrums. They were thrown aside as a sheet of white light enveloped the time machine and seemed almost to pick it up and shake it, like some giant playing dice with anything to hand. There was the sound of shattering glass. Books and papers flew across the control room. Gauges danced to a tune other than their own. Then there was a final shudder and the TARDIS settled back again.

Steven levered himself up from the floor and saw the Doctor lying flat on his back. 'Are you all right, Doctor?'

'Oh, yes,' came the reply. 'I just love games like this.'

'What was it?'

The Doctor slowly sat up and rubbed the base of his spine. 'Some sort of bomb.' He groaned a little to give vent to his feelings. 'But they needn't have bothered to try. The TARDIS can take more than that.'

'Are you sure?'

'As sure as I can be.' He grasped the edge of the control panel and pulled himself to his feet. 'When I design a shield I don't fiddle about with half measures.' He cocked his head as there came a familiar bumping and knocking through the walls. 'The little devil's come to see what the score is.'

'I wish I knew.'

'Don't worry. We're still ahead. The thing's doomed to disappointment.' As the bumping ceased he looked into the scanner, to see the Chumbley rolling away into the distance. 'Away he goes, empty-handed.'

Steven rubbed his head where it had banged on the floor in the fall. 'Given up, I suppose.'

'Or to come back with a different variety of trouble.

We'll try not to be here when it arrives, shall we?' He operated the controls and the doors moaned open. 'Come along. There isn't much time left.'

Steven followed. 'Two dawns, to be precise, which isn't enough.'

Maaga had joined Vicki at the table. Before her was a plate of greenery which she was eating, with no evidence of enjoyment. 'You're sure you won't join me?' she asked.

Vicki looked in distaste at the food. 'No, thanks. It looks like leaves to me.'

'It *is* leaves. This particular form is high in protein, without which no life form can survive. How do you propose to do so?'

'Not by eating that rubbish. Anyway, your soldiers gave me some tablet food.'

Maaga was shocked. 'You ate the same food as they do?'

'Why not?'

'Because they are slaves. And their food is suited to their status. It's inferior, enough to keep them alive and active but not to give pleasure. Our society is quite firm about what reward is given to which functionary. They are soldiers, no more, no less. I would be grateful if you would treat them as such and not give them ideas above their station.'

Vicki knew she had found a weak spot. 'You mean they're capable of having ideas? I thought you had them all bundled up, neat, tidy and mindless.'

Maaga stared at her coldly, then returned to her leaves. Vicki stood up and moved restlessly across the compartment. She was worried about the Doctor and Steven. They'd been gone for a long time. She prayed that they had come to no harm, but knew the Doctor had this unique ability to find trouble where others would notice nothing and pass on their way unharmed. Sometimes she wondered if he deliberately sought it out, or if he was some sort of magnet which unwittingly drew it to himself.

'Don't worry about your friends,' Maaga said. 'They'll be back.'

Vicki did not share her certainty. 'If the Chumblies haven't caught up with them. That's possible, isn't it?'

'I doubt if it would happen,' Maaga said calmly. 'They wouldn't let it. They'd be too worried about you.'

'Which is precisely why you kept me here.'

Maaga did not bother to turn her head. 'You seem not to trust anyone. I have told you: you are here for your own safety.'

'Yes,' Vicki snapped. 'All hostages are safe, aren't they?'

Maaga shrugged indifferently. 'If your friends are not back soon we shall go and look for them. After all, we need your help against the Rills.'

'Whether we want to give it or not.'

Now Maaga did turn and her smile reached no further in than her lips. 'I am sure you all want to help us.'

The Doctor and Steven made their way in the direction of the Drahvin spaceship, the Doctor

42

straying aside from time to time to pick the odd plant and stuff it into his pocket for later reference. Considering the circumstances, Steven found this irritating. They were on the brink of a nova and Vicki was in the clutches of the Drahvins, yet still he found time to potter. It made little sense to him. Perhaps one day he would grow used to the Doctor's ways, but he doubted it. Here was a man who was always insisting that people get their priorities right, but where were his?

'Come on, Doctor.'

'I'm with you, I'm with you.'

'This is no time for gardening.'

'Research, my boy, that's what this is.'

'With Vicki in trouble?'

'Ah, yes.'

The Doctor caught up with Steven and side by side they hastened to Vicki's rescue, until there was a loud splintering sound and the soil sagged beneath them. Then it gave way completely and they fell, clods, gravel and splintered wood going down with them. The Doctor landed on his side and his elbow shrieked agony. Steven, more fortunate, came down on his feet, only to sit abruptly as his legs gave way. Both were taken completely by surprise. It was some time before they could work out what had happened, the Doctor doing so by remaining where he was, clasping his elbow and peering dubiously about him.

The Chumblies had been busy. The Doctor and Steven were in a neatly-cut pit-trap some four metres square and a little short of four metres high. The three suns stared down at them in their bed of rubble and for a while they stared back in hopelessness. It occurred to the Doctor that they were being outsmarted on all fronts. He blamed himself. He was in charge and therefore the responsibility was his. Why did he always allow himself to be distracted by minutiae? He should have been alert and concentrating for exactly such an eventuality as this, instead of which he had allowed himself to be diverted by the flora of this planet. Well, it was time he did something. He rose slowly and painfully to his feet.

'What shall we do now?' he said.

Steven, also now on his feet, put his hands on his hips and studied their plight. 'Easily asked, Doctor, but not so easily answered. We stepped right into this, didn't we?'

'That we did.'

Steven gave a wry smile. 'The only way to get out of this is with one mighty bound. D'you think you could do that for me?'

'Alas, my boy, even I have my limitations.'

'Pity.'

Steven went to one side of the pit and examined it. He dug his hand in and pulled some of the soil away. Apart from its colour it was very much like that of Earth, a little heavier perhaps and rather more like clay, but definitely diggable. The only trouble was that they had no tools and he could not see them digging their way out with their hands. That was definitely out. He stood back and eyed the top. Then he turned and looked judgingly at the Doctor.

'I can't climb up that,' the Doctor said immediately,

44

concerned momentarily for his own welfare.

'I didn't think you could,' Steven said. 'How tall are you, Doctor?'

'Oh, five feet nine or ten. I've never measured this body. It's enough that I inhabit it.'

'And I'm about six feet.' He eyed the top of the pit again. 'I've an idea the Chumblies carved this pit to their own limitations.'

The Doctor shook his head. 'I'm not quite with you.'

'Well, if you were to stand one of them on top of the other they'd still be well below the edge, wouldn't they?'

The Doctor nodded. 'Yes.'

'But, of course, one couldn't stand on the other because they've got neither feet nor legs. Whereas we have.'

Understanding dawned in the Doctor's eyes. He snapped his fingers. 'You have it. They didn't allow for either our height or our agility. What would trap them wouldn't necessarily do the same for us.'

'I'm glad you understand.' Steven's patience was wearing thin. Somewhere in the distance he could hear the familiar chittering sound of the robots. It lent some urgency to his attitude. 'Right. I'll crouch down here against the side and you get up so that you can climb onto my shoulders.'

He did so and the Doctor scrambled awkwardly up to his position, leaning his hands against the soil in readiness.

'Now,' Steven said and slowly raised himself until he was upright, surprised at the Doctor's lack of

45

weight, even though familiar with the slightness of his appearance. For his part the Doctor felt uneasy. There was an insecurity about his feet on Steven's shoulders, despite the fact that his ankles were being firmly gripped by the young man. He never had seen himself as part of a circus act and this experience was drawing him no nearer to it. But he too could now hear the sound of the robot. His fingers scrabbled upward for the edge of the drop. He strained and grunted but could not quite reach. Black dirt spattered into his face, but still he struggled, blinking to clear his eyes and trying to keep his mouth closed as much as possible.

'Any luck?' Steven called.

'I'm a matter of inches short of it,' the Doctor replied.

'Hang on, then. I'm going to let go of your right ankle, but don't worry about it.'

He did so and the Doctor *was* worried. He wobbled uncertainly, but managed to remain upright. And suddenly he found himself being inched further up. One hand against the side of the pit to help take the strain, Steven raised himself onto his toes and somehow managed to stay there, the calves of his legs telling him that, light though the Doctor was, they were unhappy about this unusual position. 'Try that,' he grunted.

The Doctor's fingers clawed away again – and found the edge. He gasped with relief and looked upward to see if he could possibly get a grip so that he could hoist himelf, though he doubted if this ageing body could manage such a thing. Still, the effort had to be made.

What he saw above him was a Chumbley, its gun pointing in the usual direction, namely at the Doctor. But he was growing used to this and the situation was desperate. Praying that he wouldn't fall, he too inched his feet back and raised himself onto his toes. Steven's shirt began to slip on his shoulders and the Doctor felt his balance beginning to go. Sweat beaded his forehead. The last thing he could take was a fall from this height. In total desperation he lunged for the only thing he could get a grip on. This happened to be the metal skirting of the Chumbley. Inside it was a protruding rim and this the Doctor locked onto with both hands. And there he hung, staring upward with no little trepidation, suspended from this machine which was displaying no noticeable signs of friendliness.

'Are you there, Doctor?' Steven called, in some pain now and urgently needing relief.

'Heaven only knows where I am,' the Doctor replied through gritted teeth. 'But I think I'm in trouble.'

'Are you all right if I move away?'

'It makes no difference to me now.'

Steven stepped back and looked up. It was a strange sight that greeted his eyes, the weirdly-dressed Doctor hanging rigid with fear from the skirt of his metal enemy. Clearly something had to be done, and quickly. He sized up the situation and came up with the only answer.

'Have you got a firm grip, Doctor?'

'As firm as I can manage.'

'I'm going to pull hard on your ankles.'

47

'You're going to do what?' the Doctor cried.

But this was no time for argument. He grasped the Doctor's ankles, readied himself and pulled hard. The Doctor hung grimly on, convinced that he was about to lose all his fingernails. 'Have you gone mad?' he cried as he saw the Chumbley moving inch by inch over the edge.

'It's the only thing to do.'

'But you're breaking my hands.'

'Yes, yes, yes.'

Steven gave another tug and down the Doctor came, to be caught in Steven's waiting arms. But he did not fall alone. The Chumbley was teetering on the edge before their dumbstruck gaze. Its wheels spun backward and soil cascaded from them. But to no avail. There came an awesome moment when it seemed to be leaning over at some forty-five degrees, then it fell to the bottom with a great crash of metal.

Steven grinned. 'That's what I wanted.'

The Chumbley lay on its side, quite helpless, its gun snapped, wheels spinning uselessly in the air. The arms emerged from its body and it tried to lever itself up, but the effort was in vain; they weren't long enough. It was as much of a threat now as a tortoise flipped onto its back.

'Can you turn it off?' Steven asked the Doctor.

The Doctor dug about in his jacket pocket and drew out a screwdriver. 'I can try.' He looked sharply at Steven. 'Always assuming, of course, that my fingers will still work.'

Steven was offended. 'Well, we got it down, didn't we?'

The Doctor moved cautiously toward the machine. 'Almost disabling me in the process,' he added. He examined the back of the machine's headpiece. Sure enough, there was an inspection hatch there. He sighed with relief as he saw that the Rills used screws to secure such things and set to to get them out. They were tightly set but well-lubricated, so within minutes they were free and the Doctor lifted the hatch clear. Putting it aside he looked carefully at the wires, coils and other unidentifiable parts that made the robot function. He had to hand it to the Rills: they certainly were technologically advanced, sufficiently so to baffle even him initially. But it was only a matter of different means to the same end. He had encountered robots before. He would use his own advanced technique to stop the thing: that is to say, he would pull out everything within sight until his aim was achieved. Promptly he put his fingers in and did precisely that. It was quite enjoyable. Wire after wire came free under his tugging until they hung like a bunch of straw from the back of the robot's head. And finally it was still. The wheels stopped spinning, the arms gave way and it lay there dumb and, to all intents and purposes, dead.

The Doctor stepped back and surveyed his handiwork with satisfaction. 'That seems to have done it.'

'Good.' Steven put his hands beneath the robot. 'Help me get it upright, will you, Doctor?'

'Why d'you want that?'

'So that we can stand on it.'

The Doctor looked up at the top of the pit,

shrugged and also put his hands beneath the robot. It was far from being light work. The Chumbley seemed to weigh a ton and the two were gasping for breath when they finally set it upright. Once there, however, it was easy to move. Steven trundled it to the side and scraped soil under the wheels to secure them. He hoisted himself up and made sure of his footing on the head. Then he crouched and held out his hands to the Doctor. 'Right, up you come.'

The Doctor was baffled. 'What foolishness is this?'

'We get you up here, then you stand on my shoulders and climb out. It's quite simple,' Steven said patiently.

'Is it?' But he took Steven's hands nevertheless and was hoisted up, to find himself pressed face to face against the young man, with no room to move back. 'I don't like this at all.'

But Steven eased himself down to a crouching position. 'Right, Doctor. Up on my shoulders.'

Wary of falling, the Doctor scrambled up and stood with his hands against the pit side.

'Ready?'

'When you are.'

Steven gently eased himself upright and the Doctor's hands stepped their way up the side and over the top. He found himself chest and shoulders above it and climbed easily onto the surface. Immediately he lay flat and stretched out his hands to Steven. The young man took them and leapt up and over. They stood and looked down upon the disabled Chumbley.

'It seems a shame to leave it like that,' Steven said.

'Don't you worry, my boy, no-one abandons

machinery like that. His friends will be along soon to get him out.'

'*Very* soon, I should think. We'd better be on our way.'

They set off for the ship as the distant chittering of the rescue party reached their ears and speeded their steps.

The battered ship loomed above them and the Doctor paused at the entry to fish out his screwdriver again. He went to the hull and scratched through the space-dirt to the body itself. He looked closely. 'As I thought, Steven. There's nothing particularly advanced about this material. It's tough, but not impregnable. A reasonably common metal with nothing special about it.'

'So?' Steven said.

'So?' The Doctor sniffed. 'So much for *their* female scientists.'

'Biased, aren't we?'

'Amateurism never impresses me. Well, let's go and see our lady friends. It's no good you standing here admiring the scenery.'

Vicki was relieved to see them. 'What took you so long?'

'We were held up by a Chumbley,' Steven said.

'Were you hurt at all?'

'No, no, my dear.' The Doctor smiled soothingly. 'Even though it tried to blow up the TARDIS while we were in it.'

Maaga had entered while he was speaking. 'He did not succeed?'

51

'Well, of course he didn't,' the Doctor snapped. 'We're here, aren't we? And my ship isn't a piece of old tin like this.'

'It serves its purpose.'

'More or less. Frankly, I wouldn't venture anywhere in it. I'd be terrified of it falling to bits about me.'

Maaga gestured to Drahvin One who had brought them in. The minion depressed a lever and the door hummed shut. The Doctor was annoyed. 'Is that necessary?'

'We have to protect ourselves against the machines,' Maaga replied. 'But we are wasting time. Did you learn anything more about this planet?'

'Only confirming what you already know.' The Doctor saw no reason for telling the truth. 'This planet has exactly fourteen dawns to live. Then comes the big bang.'

Steven concealed his surprise at the Doctor's words. He saw no reason for the lie, but then no-one ever knew what was going on in the Doctor's mind. It was murky and devious and ploughed its own furrow, when it wasn't flying off in all directions.

'Fourteen dawns,' Maaga mused. 'Doctor, will you help us?'

'To do what, exactly?'

'To capture the Rills' spaceship so that we can escape.'

'And how do I do that, mmm? And, of course, the other question: what happens to the Rills if you succeed?'

Maaga's lips tightened. 'They stay on this planet.'

'But they'll be blown up,' Vicki protested. 'Why couldn't you take them off with you?'

Maaga was growing tired of this girl. She was not used to being questioned and doubted. Hers was to command and others to obey. Without that arrangement there could be no order. And already she was being delayed. But then, she reminded herself, she had to be civil or it was possible that this strange fellow called the Doctor would refuse to help. Of course, he could be forced, but willing co-operation would be better. She contained the snappy answer she'd been about to give. 'They are murderers and they are evil. Totally evil. If you were to see them you would know it immediately.'

'We have only your word for that,' the Doctor observed. 'But I'd better point out to you that we cannot help you at all.'

'Why not?'

'Because I kill nothing. I'm not permitted to even if I wanted to, which I don't. As for my friends here: they aren't made that way. No, no, anything involving the death of another being is out of the question.'

Maaga stared at him coldly. 'I am interested to know how your species has managed to survive this long.'

'By the use of a moral code.'

'And what is that?'

'I don't believe it,' Steven said. 'You don't know what a moral code is?'

'If I did I would not have asked the question.'

'It's – '

But he was interrupted by the Doctor. 'Never mind

53

all that. You might as well talk to a post for all the good it'll do. The point is, we are in no position to be of assistance. Now if you'd be so kind as to open that door we'll be on our way.'

'You do not fully understand the situation,' Maaga said. 'It is a very basic one: either the Rills die or we do.'

The Doctor was growing tired of such single-mindedness. In fact, he wasn't sure that it wasn't so much single as simple. Whatever it was, it was beginning to grate on his nerves. 'You could both get off together, couldn't you? Did it never occur to you that if you joined forces you'd probably be away from this planet in no time at all? Your problems would then be solved, out into space and no-one left behind.'

'Impossible.'

'What's so impossible about it?' Steven asked. 'Have you ever tried being friendly?'

'Oh, she wouldn't do that,' Vicki said scornfully. 'I reckon she *wants* to be enemies.'

'The situation was forced upon us,' Maaga replied. 'They killed one of my soldiers.'

'It could have been a mistake,' Steven pointed out. 'After all, there you were out in space and you suddenly encountered each other.' A thought occurred to him. 'Who fired first, by the way?'

'They did. They were upon us before we even knew of their presence. All we did know was that we were hit, and badly at that. Naturally, we returned their fire.'

'Naturally,' Vicki said in a voice totally lacking conviction.

54

The Doctor emerged from the reverie he had fallen into. 'There is one thing.'

'And what is that?'

'How does it come about that you know what the Rills look like? I've seen neither hide nor hair of them.'

For the first time Maaga faltered. 'We fought them on this planet. We drove them back into their space vessel and they have not emerged since, only sending their machines out on patrol.' Her expression was one of distaste. 'They are vile creatures, revolting to see and disgusting to smell. That you could even think of us befriending them is incredible.'

The Doctor eyed her beadily. 'I see. Then I'd better sum things up for you.'

'Please do.'

'Oh, I shall. Don't worry about that. And it's really very simple.' He waved a hand vaguely about him. 'All of this is not our business, not our business at all. We don't know you and we don't know the Rills either. Speaking for myself, I can't say that I particularly want to, which applies to both of you. Yet you ask for our help, with no evidence whatsoever that you've tried to help yourselves. Well, I'll tell you now, you aren't going to get it. I've never heard such nonsense in my life. Why you don't send one of your minions out to talk peace I really don't know. But since you won't, take it from me, you're on your own.'

Maaga's voice was chill. 'I have explained everything to you.'

'Not necessarily to my satisfaction.'

'What is it that would satisfy you?'

'Talking to someone with a grain of sensitivity would be a start,' the Doctor snapped. 'Talking to you is very much akin to going for a walk with a tree. Nothing moves. The response is nil. Since you can't go away, we will. Kindly open that door.'

Maaga's response was predictable. The Doctor saw it happening before it actually did. She took her handgun from her holster and pointed it at him. 'You will please change your mind.'

The Doctor shook his head. 'No.'

The atmosphere could have been sliced with a knife. Vicki and Steven looked on in tense alarm as the Doctor eyed the weapon and the woman holding it. He cared for neither. In fact his indifference was turning to active dislike. Here he was pursuing his normal life of scientific enquiry and suddenly finding himself being dragooned into what bore all the makings of an all-out war. It was all too much. Why, oh why, did these things keep happening to him? Assuming there was a God, he seemed to look upon the Doctor with an ironic eye. Benevolence would make a nice change, a spell of peace and quiet somewhere with nothing at all happening and no-one threatening his tranquillity of mind. And he had to admit that for himself: he was a serene person, not given to such trivial emotions as impatience or anger. Indeed, it sometimes crossed his mind that he could be taken as a model for all life forms to shape themselves upon. They would be the beneficiaries. So why was this stupid woman pointing this ridiculous weapon at him?

'Oh, put it away,' he said testily. 'You've no intention of using it.'

'But I have,' Maaga replied. 'You may look down on our technology, but I assure you our weapons are most efficient, as am I.'

'I'm no use to you dead. Surely you can see that.'

'No-one spoke of death.' She lowered the gun slightly. 'But if I point this at your hand and press the –'

She went no further because Steven leapt at her. He grasped the gun with both hands and wrenched it upward, thinking to snatch it from her grasp. But he was surprised by the unexpected strength of the Drahvin leader. Startled though she was, she retained an iron grip on the weapon and even started to force it down again. Steven was up to that, however. He tightened his grip, now on her knuckles, braced himself and squeezed with all his strength. Maaga gasped with pain, but still held on. Nothing in her training had taught her to accept defeat and she had no intention of learning such a lesson now. This particular intruder was a nuisance. It was time he died. Men were a burden at the best of times, as she well knew. They served no purpose other than to irritate and obstruct, as this one was doing. Time was drifting away and she had to get herself and her soldiers off the planet before it split asunder and hurled its debris into the eternity of dead space. Something had to be done, so she did it. She rammed her knee up at Steven's groin.

But he had been waiting for exactly that. Retaining his grip with one hand, he dropped the other to below her lifted knee and yanked hard. Over she went, like a toppled doll, to crash onto the deck with an ugly thud, her head connecting as well and wiping out her mind for a matter of seconds. That was enough for Steven. By the time she was blinking her way back to clarity and intending to renew the fight, he was standing over her with the gun pointed at her head. Beside him was Vicki, clutching a drink container that she had obviously intended to use for purposes other than that for which it was designed. Maaga felt no fear, but duty had to be borne in mind: her duty was to get her ship and soldiers into space or, short of her ship, that of the Rills. To do that she had to remain alive. Yet there were several ways of achieving that end.

She narrowed her eyes calculatingly. 'You would not dare kill me.'

Steven smiled. It was not a nice smile – it lacked warmth. 'Try me.'

The Doctor could see that the young man was not in the best of moods. He rather fancied that, pushed too far, he might do something foolish. Something decisive was called for. 'Let's go,' he said, 'while there's still time.'

Steven backed away, his knuckle showing too white on the gun. Maaga lay still, deciding she had pushed matters as far as they would go. The man looked nervous. From such a state of mind evil things can come. She might get damaged and that would do no good for her crew. Best to leave things as they stood. 'You *will* help us,' was as much as she could muster.

'Place no bets,' Steven said, his brain still in a turmoil of rage. He knew he hated the woman and he knew that it was not just because she had proved so strong, but he really disliked her and the temptation to do her a serious injury was almost irresistible. If he yielded to it, he would feel a lot better. But not later, he reminded himself, not later. Then would come the misgivings, the remorse. Never before in his life had he fought a woman. It was not an experience he would choose to repeat. Yet his finger still itched on the trigger. He viewed the supine Maaga and said, very gently, 'The next time we run across each other, step aside. My good breeding is leaving me.'

Maaga only stared at him – and loathed him.

'Come on, come on,' the Doctor said from the entry. 'We can't afford to idle away our time like this.'

'All right,' Steven replied, and moved towards the door.

Vicki crossed to the Doctor who pressed the door lever. It slid open – and there were the three Drahvins, returned from patrol and still holding their guns, which happened yet again to be pointed at the Doctor. Their faces were as devoid of expression as ever they were, but there was no arguing with the outlets of their weapons. The Doctor surveyed them bleakly: such beauty, yet no being behind it. He would have felt sorry for them, but time was running short. 'Step aside,' he said. 'We're leaving.'

Drahvin One opened her pretty mouth and spoke. 'You are not. We await instructions from Maaga.'

Maaga rose to her feet and held out a hand to Steven: 'My gun.'

Reluctantly he handed it over. She took it and put it in her holster. 'Now you will help us.'

'We don't seem to have a lot of choice,' the Doctor said.

'You have none at all. The Rills have fourteen dawns in which to repair their spaceship.' She paused as she saw Steven glance at the Doctor. 'It *is* fourteen, isn't it?'

The Doctor nodded vigorously. 'Absolutely.'

She eyed him suspiciously. 'You're quite sure?'

'Quite.'

'Suddenly I don't believe you.' Her voice sharpened. 'When is the explosion due to occur?'

'As I said. In fourteen dawns' time.'

Maaga made a gesture and Drahvins One and Two crossed to Vicki and seized her. 'Let go of me,' she said. But their grip was firm and she stilled when she saw Drahvin Three aiming her gun at her.

'If you don't tell me the truth we shall kill the girl,' Maaga said. There was no emotion in her voice. She had stated a fact and that was all there was to it.

The Doctor could do nothing but concede the point. It was obvious that the threat was a real one. 'Very well. We have two dawns left.'

Maaga was clearly shaken. 'Is that all?'

'Yes. My calculations were exact.'

Maaga pulled herself together. 'Then you don't have a lot of time in which to capture the Rills' ship.' She pointed. 'It is that way. It will not take you long to find.'

The Doctor was taken aback. 'Just like that? You expect us to stroll over there, announce that we're in charge and the Rills will simply surrender?'

'I do not care what method you use. I need that ship and I shall have it.'

'It may not be repaired yet.'

I'll bet it isn't,' Steven said. 'If it were they'd have gone by now, wouldn't they?'

'I am quite sure the Doctor can make good any damage still remaining. And you have one advantage: the Rills believe they have fourteen dawns left. We know differently. That being so, you had better be off. The girl will stay here.'

'No, she won't,' Steven said. 'I will.'

'You will go with the Doctor.'

He shook his head. 'Nope. Vicki can.'

The Doctor could see that Steven had something in mind, though he did not know what. 'If you want us to help you'll do as the young man says, or no-one goes anywhere.'

Maaga hesitated, but she was aware that time was passing. She nodded. 'Very well. The girl can go with you.'

Vicki sighed with relief. She had no idea of what the Doctor could possibly do, but anything would be better than incarceration with Maaga and her three morons. She did not know why Steven had been so insistent about remaining, but he was no fool and she presumed his reasons were good.

'Come along, Vicki,' the Doctor said as he headed for the door.

Drahvin Three operated the lever to open the door and the Doctor and Vicki went outside, both nodding a farewell to Steven who grinned at them. 'Don't get into any mischief,' he said. The door closed behind his friends and he turned back to Maaga. 'Surely you don't think they'll be able to capture the Rills' spaceship, do you?'

61

Maaga surveyed him coldly. 'If they do not we shall all die together.'

The Doctor stood outside the spaceship and looked thoughtfully into the sky. He had the curious feeling that he had missed something – something that was staring him right in the face. What could it be? He let his mind thread very gently through the experiences they had had since materialising on this planet; he was not concentrating too hard, and in fact noticed that one of the suns had now gone down and the next was edging toward the horizon. Their speed of travel he did not know, but clearly night could not be far away. How long that would last he had no idea, but guessed not too long. By the time the last sun had gone down the first would be moving round to rise again and that would bring the planet one step nearer to extinction. What was it that chap Bertrand Russell had said? Something about the fact that the Earth's sun having risen for countless millions of years being no guarantee that it would rise tomorrow. That man knew of what he spoke. In life it was all too easy to take matters for granted and assume that things would trundle along as they always had. But where was the guarantee? Fate had a nasty habit of lulling beings into a false sense of security and then yanking the mat from under them. It had happened before and would undoubtedly go on doing so. It was about to happen here, with quite a sizeable bang. He found himself wishing that he could retain his own mind and this time occupy a body more like Steven's, compact, muscular, capable of far more than this decrepit creation he was using at the moment. He was tired of it. Sooner or later renewal would come and he prayed that when the time came he would be better served. Something comfortable and capable was what he longed for, something able to do more of what he asked of it. He mused and pondered on the whimsical ways of Fate.

'Where have you gone, Doctor?' Vicki asked softly. She had seen him trekking through his own mind before and knew better than to jolt him. He usually came up with something.

'Ah.' The Doctor collected his straying thoughts. 'I was wondering how long the night lasts,' he lied. 'Not very long, by the looks of it.'

'Shouldn't we be getting on?'

'A few hours at most,' he continued. 'The question is, how long is the intervening day?'

'Not long enough, considering what's going to happen.'

'Quite, quite.' The Doctor was about to turn away when his eye was caught by the scratches his screwdriver had made in the hull of the ship near the door. He looked closer and sighed at his own slowness. There it was, staring him right in the face. Sometimes he wondered how he had survived as long as he had. Was it pure luck, or did he have a personal guardian angel looking after him? 'Do you remember when we were captured by that . . . Chumbley?' he asked.

'I'm not likely to forget it in a hurry,' Vicki said.

'And that gun it had which fired some sort of light ray?'

'Yes, of course.'

The Doctor still gazed at the scratches. 'Quite powerful, wasn't it?'

Vicki was puzzled. 'It certainly looked it.'

'Then why haven't they used it on this ship?' the Doctor mused. 'After all, if the Rills are such enemies of the Drahvins why don't they just wipe them out?'

'Perhaps the rays won't penetrate metal.'

'Oh, they could. 'I'd guess that a ray as powerful as that would cut through this ship as though it were made of butter.'

Vicki looked along the hull. All she could see were the scars of the battle in space. Yet even they proved something: that the Rills had weapons capable of a fair amount of destruction. Yet they had not used them at close quarters. She shrugged the puzzle away. There was probably a good reason, though she could not even guess at it. 'Shouldn't we be going?'

'Yes, yes, by all means.'

They set off in the direction indicated by Maaga, with no idea of what they would find or how they would cope with it. Yet, as was usual with the Doctor, all that could be done was to press on. He did so, his eyes bright with curiosity. Offered no choice, Vicki went with him.

Steven sat at the table and pondered on the Drahvins. Such beautiful creatures, yet so totally lacking in warmth. It seemed to him a shameful waste. What sort of being wilfully created women like these? They were fit only to obey orders and that was probably their only reason for existing at all. Still, he supposed it was better to have mindless minions rather than intelligent ones who might start asking awkward questions. The better the mind, the more likely it was to start trouble, a fact well known to all dictators on Earth, who had long made it their practice to take the minds of the young and manipulate them to their own devious ends. Freedom of thought can have dangerous consequences. They never allowed any such thing.

He was achieving nothing by silence. He addressed Drahvin Three who chanced to be nearest. 'D'you mind if I have some food? I'm famished.'

She glanced at him coolly, then crossed to a cabinet and took out a tin. From this she shook out two tablets and dropped them into his outstretched palm. 'Eat.'

'No, no,' he said. 'You misunderstand. I haven't got a headache. I'm hungry.'

'That is our food. It is good.'

He looked down at the pills and felt his hunger leaving him. There was no way in the world those things were going to do him any good. What he felt more inclined to was a good beef roast with potatoes and greens on the side and plenty of gravy, preferably followed up by something light, such as strawberries and cream. What good were these things? He looked gloomily up at Drahvin Three. 'I'll bet Maaga doesn't eat these.'

'No. She is our leader.'

'Then I'll try what she has, if you don't mind.'

'You cannot. It is food for leaders only.'

He stared narrowly into the vacancy of her face. 'That doesn't seem very fair, does it?'

She was confused. 'Fair?'

65

He began to feel that he was achieving something, however slight. The thing to do was to keep going while he had the edge, to try and stir up a little resentment, if possible. 'Why should she have special food while you have to eat junk like this?'

She looked at the tablets. 'It is food.'

'Oh, sure,' he needled. 'Great stuff. I can see it going down well with a touch of salt and vinegar, or perhaps a little salad dressing. I suppose Maaga has lots of other special things as well?'

'She is our leader and has leader's things.'

'Like what?' he asked.

'Her gun, her food, her –'

'Her gun?' he cut in.

Drahvin Three nodded. 'A leader's gun can destroy anything.'

'Even the Chumblies?'

'I do not understand.' It was a statement of fact. No confusion showed on her face and nor did anything else.

'The machines,' he said. 'The robots. Those things that keep banging about here all the time, trying to get at you.'

'They too can be destroyed.'

'Then surely it would be better if you all had these guns. You wouldn't have to fear the machines then, would you?'

'There is only one. Maaga has it because she is the leader.'

Her logic, he felt, was impeccable. She had obviously been reared to believe in only one set of values and anything not fitting was to be dismissed.

66

Well, if Maaga and her companions could do it, why shouldn't he try the same? After all, there was little to be lost and a good deal to gain if he could disrupt this cosy little arrangement. 'You could use it when you went out on patrol though.'

She gave an almost imperceptible pause. 'Yes.'

'Then doesn't it seem right that you should?'

The curtain came down again. 'Only if Maaga says so.'

Steven sighed inwardly. Always he came up against the brick wall that was Maaga and her rules. There had to be a way round it, but he was not having much luck in finding it. Still, he thought, onward. 'If you took it and went out against the machines and destroyed one, then Maaga would be pleased with you.'

'She would.'

'Then you should take her gun and that would make her happy.' He spoke as though to a child, which he estimated she pretty well was. He held out his hand. 'Give me your gun while you go and get hers, then we'll destroy the machines together.'

'Yes.'

She held out the gun and a disbelieving Steven was about to snatch it when Maaga's voice cut in from the doorway. 'You are trying to be too clever.' She entered and confronted Drahvin Three. 'You have done badly. You will be punished. This is a prisoner, not to be spoken to.'

The Drahvin's face paled. 'He was talking.'

'He was trying to trick you, just as the machines do. The only words you need to hear are those I utter.'

Three bowed her head. 'I was wrong. I did not understand.'

'Go to your quarters.'

The Drahvin left. The other two remained quite still. Maaga turned on Steven, her voice still harsh. 'You will keep out of our way.'

'Gladly,' he said. 'I don't particularly want to be here at all.'

She paused and looked at him shrewdly. 'You don't have to be. You could easily escape.'

'Could I?' he said, very much on his guard.

'Yes, in your own ship.'

'Ah, I see. And, of course, I'd be taking you lot along as companions.'

'You would hardly expect us to remain here.'

'Well, I'll tell you something.' He put his hands in his pockets and deliberately slouched his shoulders in an attempt to appear helpless, which as far as such a proposition was concerned he was. 'Even assuming that I believed you and that you didn't decide along the way that I was eating too much food, there is a snag.'

'And what is that?'

'I can't operate it, couldn't if I tried for ever. Only the Doctor can do that. He designed it and he controls it. But I have a suggestion to make. Why don't you put the offer to him? Or do you think he might be too smart for you?' Steven smiled. 'I may look the part of the gullible one, but I can't help you at all.'

'I could make you,' she snapped.

'No, you couldn't. You've never seen the inside of the TARDIS. It's bulging with instruments. I wouldn't even know where to start. I'd push everything within sight and probably blow us all to Kingdom Come.'

She glared at him in frustration and pointed to a padded area in the corner. 'Get over there and stay there in silence.'

'That's an order, is it?'

'It is.'

He shrugged indifferently and crossed to where she had indicated, dwelling upon the fact that she was not as single-minded as he had thought. So, killing was not her main instinct; right alongside it was self-preservation, which was nice to know because out of that could come fear and he would very much like to see her with a touch of that. It would do him a power of good. He sat down, then decided that while he was at it he might as well lie, so he did, turning his head away from the Drahvins and closing his eyes.

There was silence for a while, then he heard them cross to the table and sit. The silence descended again until one of them finally spoke. 'Maaga?'

'What is it?'

'Why do we not kill him now?'

'I will let you kill him when I am ready.'

'Thank you, Maaga.'

Vicki and the Doctor lay prone on the ledge and looked down. The air chittered with the sound of several Chumblies and now they could see them. There was a purpose about their movements. Each covered a certain distance until it met another Chumbley, then each turned about and re-covered the

69

ground until it met another coming toward it. The same thing, over and over again. They were sentries standing guard, and very efficiently at that. The Doctor was impressed. He admired the smoothness of their motion over the jagged landscape on what had to be telescopically suspended wheels and the precision of their repeated meeting and turning. This, added to the fact that all moved at exactly the same speed, would have qualified them for duty at Buckingham Palace, it seemed to him. He smiled to himself at the thought of a bearskin set atop the head of each of them.

'We'll never get past them' Vicki muttered. They're all over the place.'

But the Doctor was still gazing at the robots. He found them fascinating. 'I wonder what the operating principle is? Relatively simple, I should think, once you knew it.'

'Doctor!' she said.

'Mmm, what is it, child?'

'How are we going to get past them?'

'Yes, a good question.' He still stared at the Chumblies. 'And one to which I don't have an immediate answer, so try to be patient. We have to observe, note, collate, then conclude. In that way we might find one.'

'We don't have an awful lot of time.'

'That much I know.' He nodded to the side. 'Look, there's another.'

She followed his gaze and saw the machine moving in their direction, soon to pass beneath them. She had had enough of this. Time was passing and each second took them one beat nearer to the end. And there was something about the Chumblies that had caught her attention. They were always face on to a target, always having to turn in order to get to the right position. It made for a certain awkwardness in their otherwise smooth mobility. A theory began to form in her head. Glancing at the Doctor she saw that he was still absorbed in the oncoming machine. She reached out and pulled a sizeable rock to her side where the Doctor could not see it. Then she, too, waited.

The Chumbley came on, was directly below them, then moved away. Vicki jumped to her feet, held the rock high above her head, then hurled it down behind the robot. It did not even pause but simply went on its way.

'What the devil are you doing?' the Doctor demanded in some agitation.

'Testing a theory,' she replied.

'Then don't. You could get us both killed.'

'But don't you see, Doctor?' she sighed. 'We were in no danger at all. The Chumblies only have sensors or whatever they are on their fronts. Anything behind them they aren't aware of at all. After all, that one didn't flicker, did it? But the rock was big enough to make anybody jump. So for as long as we can stay behind them they won't even know we're there.'

The Doctor narrowed his eyes in thought, then nodded: 'You know, I think you're right. But it was still a foolish chance to take.'

'It wasn't a chance. I noted, observed, collated and concluded, just as you said.' She grinned. '*Then* I threw the rock.'

71

He gave her a hard look. 'I'll give you the benefit of the doubt. But it means we're going to have to run for it again. I seem to have done little else since we got here. If we take that one at the end we'll stand a fair chance. Then we'll duck down to that track because that, I think, is where the spaceship is.'

They waited until the end Chumbley had turned, then did as the Doctor had said, running up behind it and stepping lightly in its track. A hiss from the Doctor and they sprinted for the opening he had indicated, just making it before the Chumbley turned to make its way back. Out of breath again, the Doctor led Vicki a short way down the gap until there before them was the Rills' base.

They halted and surveyed it. The ship itself was a vast black sphere rearing up into the sky. Here and there were observation ports and one large patch where the Drahvins had scored their direct hit. It had been repaired and stood out clearly against the matt grey of the hull. At the base of the ship the Doctor could discern vents for whatever form of propulsion was used. But, more interestingly, built onto the side of the ship was a building of quarried black rock, looking very much like a pillbox left over from a war. In front of that was some machinery which the Doctor judged to be a drill rig. He wondered what the Rills could be drilling for. Whatever it was it had to be important for them to go to such pains in constructing the building. He imagined the robots had done it. His admiration for them grew. Their designers must have been brilliant to make them capable of so many tasks. Compared with the lack of evidence of activity on the

Drahvin ship these beings had been very busy indeed. He hoped he would meet them, rather than be gunned down on sight for his troubles.

'What can they be after?' he said.

Vicki was equally puzzled. 'Oil? Gas?'

'Difficult to say. Well, there's only one way to find out.'

But they had to duck out of sight as a Chumbley emerged from one of the narrow entries in the building. It stopped, rotated its head from side to side, then went back in again. As soon as it had gone Vicki and the Doctor hastened across to where it had stood. The Doctor's eye was caught by a grill set low in the wall. He stopped and examined it.

'An air vent?' Vicki guessed. 'Or some sort of purifier?'

'More than that, I think.' He put his hand against it. 'It's drawing air in. It could be for converting air into something else.'

'Like what?'

'Heaven only knows. Come on, let's go in and pray we don't run into one of your Chumblies.'

He led the way through the entry and they found themselves in a passageway. Like the outside it was excellently and strongly constructed, either because that was the way the Rills always did things or because they feared the possibility of attack. And there was a peculiarly pungent odour on the air. The Doctor sniffed and looked a query at his companion.

Vicki nodded. 'Yes, I can smell it too and I can't place it, though I know I ought to be able to.'

'Then let's find out.'

73

They moved on down the passageway, hearing Chumblies moving about in the building and smelling the odour growing stronger. They emerged into a large space. Three of the walls were of rock, but the fourth was grey, clearly the side of the space vessel. Here and there, neatly stacked, were various constructional pieces and repair equipment. The Doctor looked about him at the numerous entries to the area. This was obviously the working centre. He looked at one of the stacks. 'Look, part of a robot. They must repair each other.'

'Yes. I know what that smell is now, Doctor.'

'Oh?'

'Ammonia.'

'So it is. Interesting . . .' He moved to the side of the spaceship and looked hard at it. 'Well, I don't need to try my screwdriver on that. A very superior metal. Beautiful. Hardly a metal at all, in fact. Wonderful material for a spaceship. I wonder how far they travelled to wind up here?'

'Very far, do you think?'

'That depends on their means of propulsion. But I would think it's pretty advanced, because a ship built like this is easily capable of hopping from one galaxy to another.'

'Like us,' she said.

'Like *me*,' he corrected her.

And suddenly Vicki screamed and pointed in horror. 'Doctor, look!'

3

Airlock

Rigid with fear, Vicki stared at the side of the Rills'
spaceship. The Doctor followed her gaze and was
greatly interested. A shutter had slid aside. Behind it
was a somewhat bigger observation port and behind
that two huge, heavily-lidded eyes were watching
them. They looked like soft pools of concern, dark
brown and gentle. What they could see of the face
surrounding them, which was bigger than the port,
was a scaly coat resembling that of a lizard. Around
this vision swirled thick strands of ammonia gas.

'What is it?' Vicki gasped.

'At a guess, my dear, that is a Rill.' The Doctor
moved closer and looked into the eyes that looked into
his. 'Yes, I'd say I'm right. What I'm looking at is
intelligence, and considerable at that. Come and have
a look for yourself.'

Vicki shuddered. 'No, thank you. And I'll tell you
now, I find it difficult to believe that an animal like
that has "considerable intelligence".'

'Animal?' The Doctor tutted to himself. 'No
intelligence indeed. When will you learn that not all
life forms are structured like man? Some are better,

some not. But they all have one thing in common: they've learned to adapt. And sometimes from that adaptation comes intelligence, as in this case.'

'But that scaly head!'

'What of it?'

'It's horrid!'

'I do hope it isn't listening to you,' the Doctor said reprovingly. 'For all you know, it finds our appearance revolting. I can't think why it shouldn't. *I'm* not too fond of mine.'

'It's a good deal better than that.'

'A charming if somewhat back-handed compliment.' He returned his gaze to the eyes, to see again what Vicki could not, the high intelligence. The eyelids blinked only every fifteen or so seconds, coming down like purple blinds in a most leisurely manner and contrasting oddly with the green scales, to open again equally as calmly. He wondered what it made of them. Whatever it was, the Rill showed no alarm, which indicated to the Doctor that either it knew no fear or felt quite secure where it was. He wished he could communicate, but knew that no sound, however loud, could penetrate the ship's walls. It seemed a pity. He put his hands together and bowed slightly to indicate that he came in peace. Nothing happened. He repeated the gesture and again the response was nil. He sighed. 'I'm afraid it doesn't speak our language. I might as well beat my head against a brick wall. Such a pity. I know I could learn something worthwhile from it.'

'It seems to me you're presuming too much,' Vicki said dustily.

The Doctor turned to her with raised eyebrows. 'And what, pray, do you know of other life forms? Is your experience so vast that you can tell me what I can see and what I can't? Have you been a time-traveller so long?'

Vicki was put down. 'Sorry, Doctor. But I do find it very frightening.'

'Then don't. If you stumble through life believing that anything that doesn't look like you is necessarily bad you'll make a very poor fist of it. A little more tolerance is what you need and much less of this burgeoning female arrogance I seem to be encountering all the time since we landed. Claims of superiority I always find extremely boring. There's always someone better – except in my case, of course.'

Vicki knew he was only half ribbing her. The other half was intended as a salutary lesson. She hung her head, only to lift it again in a listening attitude. 'I think there's a Chumbley coming.'

The Doctor heard it too, the chittering growing louder as it approached. 'This way. Quickly.'

He led the way to an entry leading away from the sound and they bolted into it. They came to a dead halt at the sight of another machine heading straight for them, turned and rushed back into the chamber to take another way out. Finding one that seemed safe they raced into that and along the passageway. Short as the distance was, it seemed to take them forever before they saw daylight ahead.

'Come on, come on,' the Doctor panted. 'They'll be on us in a minute.'

He shot out into the waning daylight and turned for

Vicki who had fallen behind, despite her younger legs. She was only seconds behind, but they were some two too many. Just as she was about to reach the exit a heavy metal grill crashed down before her. The Doctor looked on in consternation as she banged into it, taken too much by surprise to stop. Her face suddenly white, she grasped the entrapping bars. 'Doctor!' she cried in desperate fear.

The Doctor stepped forward and examined the bars. They looked solid, but he wrenched at them just the same. They were immovable and now the sound of the pursuing Chumbley was very close. 'Hang on, Vicki,' he said, looking about for anything that might help. His eye fell on a grill like the one he had examined on the way in. He was certain now that it was a converter for the ammonia gas the Rills needed for survival, so if he could not save Vicki immediately he might be able to in the long term with the aid of a little sabotage. Fishing out his screwdriver he crossed to the grill and started to unfasten it. The screws, tight at first, began to wind out. He grunted with satisfaction, aware of the need for speed.

'Doctor, they're nearly here,' Vicki said anxiously.

'I'm aware of that.'

'What are you doing there?'

'Trying to interfere with our big-eyed friend's well-being,' he said, moving on to the next screw. 'Just try to stay calm.'

'Calm?' Her voice was climbing with fear. 'I'd much rather you had another go at these bars.'

'A complete waste of time.' This screw was also coming free. 'They're as solid as rock, whereas this

78

will do a lot more damage – eventually.'

'I think that's too late,' she said in a small voice. 'They've arrived.'

The Doctor looked up and through the bars to see Vicki still clinging on to them, but a Chumbley now beside her and pointing its gun in the usual meaningful way. 'Ah, yes,' he said. 'Whatever you do, don't make any sudden moves.'

'I'm not likely to,' she said.

The Chumbley moved forward and nudged against her legs. She clung on to the bars and it did it again. Vicki clutched even tighter. 'I think it wants me to go with it.'

The Doctor was philosophical. 'Then your wisest course is to go.'

'But that thing in there. I don't think I can bear to see it again.'

'Don't look.'

'I'm frightened,' she wailed.

'Listen to me, my dear,' he said in a low voice as the machine nudged her yet again. 'If you go along quietly and cause no trouble I've a feeling they won't harm you. But play for time so that I can help you. I'm sure I can do something with this converter, but I need more than a couple of minutes in which to do it. Now be brave and do as I say, there's a good girl.'

She nodded stiffly and released her grasp on the bars. 'You will be as quick as you can, won't you?'

'Depend on it.'

She moved away down the passage, taking small and reluctant steps. The Chumbley went behind her, chittering so loudly now that it could almost be taken as crowing with triumph, though it occurred to the Doctor that it only seemed that way because such a small passage acted as an echo chamber. He watched until they vanished, then turned back to his work, conscious of what he had not said to Vicki: that he had no idea what might happen to her.

Steven lay in the padded corner and pretended he was sleeping, even though he had not dozed for a moment. He thought it better that way. Since he was not allowed to speak he might learn something by being silent, though he was inclined to doubt it. Maaga would reveal nothing of importance in his hearing and the others were privy to nothing. It was all very strange and all very well for the Doctor. He was used to whistling about through space and time like a demented flea and encountering weird life forms such as these were turning out to be, but he and Vicki were not. Steven did not think he would ever get used to it. Too many things occurred at the same time and most of them turned out to be troublesome. Nearly always the Doctor remained calm, interested and calculating, but even he was prone to tetchiness in certain circumstances. It was not unknown for him even to lose his temper. In fact it was becoming a familiar spectacle. Sometimes he was short on tolerance.

Steven's thoughts were interrupted by the voice of Drahvin Two, still standing beside One near the bulkhead. 'Maaga, shall we go?'

Steven watched as Maaga turned from examining her charts. 'Where?'

'To patrol.'

'I see no need.'

'We might be able to find out what his two friends are doing.'

'No,' Maaga snapped. 'And besides, it is dark. You would see nothing.'

Drahvin Two looked at the ship's chronometer, her voice as monotonous as that of a speak-your-weight machine. 'We always go out on patrol at this time.'

'But you are not going now. I made the routine for you to work to and I shall change it as and when I choose. You do not question my orders, you simply obey them. Anything else brings punishment, as you know.'

The two Drahvins exchanged uneasy glances with Drahvin Three, still on guard beside Steven.

Maaga moved away from her charts and surveyed her minions with contempt. 'Soldier Drahvins! You cannot understand anything, can you? You're made unintelligent and you remain that way all your lives. Why they insisted I bring you with me I shall never understand.'

Nor did she. She had emerged from her interview with the Minister for Offensive Research with the distinct impression that she was to be a sacrificial beast. Very smooth, the Minister had been, wearing the scarlet garments of the élite and with a half-convincing expression of trust on her face. But Maaga herself was one of the élite and wore the same dress when she was not in space. She knew that one member of the class was as capable of deception as the next and she had little regard for politicians anyway. They were always full of promises which were as empty of realisation as an upended bucket was of water. They cajoled, persuaded, scratched that back and bit this one and when things went wrong could always find something beyond their control to blame it on. And none of it mattered a pinch anyway. There was only one political party, so all votes cast served only to prolong the same régime.

Not that she cared a great deal one way or the other. Her work was in space and that was all that really mattered to her. But to be sent out with a crew of soldiers was insufferable. The Minister might as well have condemned her to indefinite exile on a barren planet for all the sense and companionship she got out of them. She admitted the necessity for them on Drahva. They functioned well, or as well as could be expected, but to send them into space was a nonsense. Their ability to reason was as close to nil as it was possible to get without actually hitting it, so the task of keeping the ship out and on course fell almost entirely on her shoulders. And she was growing tired of it.

She had told the Minister that they were useless for space work, but had only received the reply that there were no other members of the élite she could spare for so long. Drahva was in crisis and all were busy with their own tasks. She had to do what she could. Maaga had experienced great difficulty in containing herself. All the damned soldiers were suitable for was the performance of elementary chores, or for killing. Beyond that their tiny brains could not reach. They understood fear of the élite and nothing else.

'To conquer space,' the Minister had said, 'you will

need soldiers. I will see that you have them.'

Well, she had done that and here was Maaga, engaged in a war and having, of all things, to depend upon males for help. It was incredible that she should have to turn to what were upon her planet mere slaves whose functions were severely curtailed. More than that, it was absurd. She was prepared to concede that the one they called Doctor gave evidence of intelligence, but the one lying there now seemed little more than an obstructive idiot, serving no more purpose than a Drahvin slave. There was no-one with whom she could share her thoughts and therein lay the nub of the problem: she had to think this war through alone. In the meantime she took exception to the fact that they were almost questioning her. She wondered if the disruptive one lying down had caused this with his wheedling, whining insinuations. She would have to do something about him soon, that was plain. In the meantime order must be maintained.

She turned on her subordinates. 'Certain things you must accept. You are bred to do so.' Her voice hardened. 'I am your commander, am I not? I am your controller.'

'Yes, Maaga,' said Drahvin Two.

'And my orders are to be obeyed.'

'Yes, Maaga.'

'Why?'

'Because you are our leader.'

'And?'

'You think.'

'And you don't know what that means.'

The two Drahvins stood in rigid silence, because

indeed they did not. The reasons behind Maaga's actions and words were beyond them. Their minds were as tranquil as puddles of oil, disturbed only occasionally by a stab of fear, and that caused only by Maaga herself.

'Very well,' Maaga said. 'At least you understand that. Now understand this. There will be no patrol until I say so. We have a prisoner. Your duty is to guard him, because in order to save him the other two must give us assistance.'

'May I speak, Maaga?' asked Drahvin One.

'If you must.'

'I do not understand why they would want to rescue a friend.'

'I do not suppose you do.'

The slight faculty Drahvin One had for thought crawled its way blindly through the empty whiteness of her mind. It found something and grasped at it. 'We would not. We would leave her.'

Maaga nodded. 'Yes, we would. But I have heard of beings like these. They help each other.'

'Why, Maaga?'

'I do not know. But sometimes, I am told, they even die for each other.'

Drahvin Three looked up. 'Die? For each other?'

'Yes. There are many strange things in the universe.'

Drahvin Two said flatly, 'I do not understand.'

Maaga sighed. The company of these idiots was beginning to grate on her nerves. If she tried to explain anything to them, even in the simplest of terms, it barely impinged upon their consciousness.

How she hated them. 'I know you don't understand,' she shouted in frustration. 'But despite that, *you will obey orders*!' She paused as all three bowed their heads, then went on, speaking almost to herself. 'It may turn out that we shall not have the chance to kill either the Rills or these Earth creatures, at least not with our own hands. It occurs to me that perhaps it would be better to escape in the Rills' spaceship and leave them here. Then, when we are out in space, we can look back. We will see a vast, white, exploding planet. And we will know they have died with it.'

'But we will not see them die,' Drahvin One said.

'*You* will not. But I, at least, will have enough intelligence to imagine it. The fear, the terror, the shuddering of a planet at the end of its life. And they will be gone, while we are out in space and free. But that is for later.' She pointed at Drahvin One: 'You will lie down and rest.' Then at Two: 'You will watch and wait for the Earthmen. And you,' turning to Three, 'will remain on guard over him.'

Drahvin One left for the inner room, Two crossed to an observation port, gun at the ready, and Three remained beside Steven. Maaga moved to look down at Steven.

'He sleeps,' said Drahvin Three.

'But you will not.'

Three nodded obedience and Maaga crossed to the inner room to have a brief rest herself. Steven squinted up at his guard. Her set face and the gun in her hands promised little good for his future.

Vicki was now being escorted by two Chumblies, the

85

original one nudging from behind and another backing away in front, its gun trained on her. In this way they traversed the passageway, Vicki's heart thumping with dread at the thought of seeing the Rill again. Why had she not kept up with the Doctor, in which case she would be free now? The fact was that she had spent too much time looking over her shoulder and therefore bumping into the passage walls and she was now paying for it. Had she done as the Doctor had and simply run for it she would not be in this pickle. His aim had been simple: to get out. She had allowed herself to be distracted by fear.

The leading Chumbley backed in to the central chamber and Vicki reluctantly followed, her eyes averted from the viewport of the Rills' ship. The less she saw of that the better. She was in no hurry to be presented with that sight again. But she could not resist stealing a quick glance. She sighed with relief when she saw the shutter was now sealed. At least that was something, not exactly a major step forward, but a source of relief, though she knew that sooner or later she would have to face up to it again. Postponement did no harm.

The Chumblies chittered and chinked for a minute or two while she waited in cold anticipation, then from the one in front of Vicki came the high-pitched sound she had heard before. It ceased. Silence fell. Vicki waited. She did not know if she was supposed to do something or not. If she was they would have to clarify. With those guns threatening her she had no intention of making any move at all, lest it be misinterpreted. That way lay the possibility of pain.

Again the high-pitched sound emanated from the Chumbley and yet again it stopped as suddenly as it had started. This time the machine twittered at her; it seemed to be waiting. Waiting for what, she wondered. Should she do a soft-shoe shuffle and hope for the best, or perhaps give them a quick burst of Shakespearian oratory? But the brief flash of gallows humour left her when the other Chumbley started persistently to nudge her from behind. What did it want now? She put up with it for as long as her patience would allow, then rounded upon it angrily: 'Don't do that! What do you want with me, anyway?'

At once the Chumbley ceased the nudging. Its lights began to flash in the visor and a series of strange sounds came from it. There were grunts, whistles, warbles, even shouts and she thought she detected what seemed to be a word or two somewhere amid the babble. Whatever the way of it, things seemed to be moving no further forward. All she could do was watch and wait while the Chumbley went through its self-inflicted agonies.

This, too, finally came to an end and all the lights stopped flashing, except one. This was bright orange and fixed her with its glare. Then, to her surprise, words came from it, much too quickly, almost tripping over each other as she barely made them out: 'Don't do that, what do you want anyway, don't do that, what do you want anyway don't do that what do you want anyway don't do that what do you want anyway.'

'That's much too fast,' she said. At last they might be getting somewhere, though where Heaven only knew. 'If you go more slowly I might be able to understand.'

'That's much too fast more slowly that's much too fast more slowly more slowly, more slowly, more slowly, more ... slowly .... more ..... slowly ...... m-o-r-e .... s–l–o–w—l—y ....'

It sounded for all the world like an old-fashioned hand-wound gramophone winding down, the voice growing deeper and deeper until it sounded as though it came from the grave.

She was in no mood to communicate with the dead. For all she knew she was about to join them anyway, so contact now would be superfluous. 'That's too slow,' she said. 'I won't be able to understand that either.'

The Chumbley chattered to itself for a moment, then spoke in measured tones: 'That's too slow. I won't be able to understand that either.'

'You've got it!' she exclaimed. 'That's more or less the right speed. Can you do anything better than repeat what I'm saying?'

The machine fell silent for a moment, then chattered to itself, stopped, then spoke. 'I think so. Yours is a difficult language, but we have processed it and should be able to comm-uni-cate. Yes, we have it now. I shall talk to you.'

'Good. Now perhaps you'll tell me why you've forced me in here.'

'You came of your own choice.'

'And we were leaving the same way until you brought the gate down on me and cut me off.'

'We are sorry to separate you from your friend, but it was necessary.'

'To you, or to me?'

The shutter slid gently down and her heart almost stopped as she saw the huge eyes surveying her. It was not the eyes, but the scales about them that she found so fearsome. Reptiles had always given her the horrors and this one was no exception, especially bearing in mind the probable size of it. But she forced herself to return the stare, a cold shiver running up her spine as the purple eyelids gently closed, paused, then drifted blandly up again. 'Who are you?' she demanded.

'Who are *you*?' came from the Chumbley.

Vicki hesitated, wondering how much she should give away. Well, the truth would possibly do no harm. 'We're . . . we're time travellers from the planet Earth.'

The huge liquid eyes seemed to be absorbing her. 'I see. But you were sent here by the Drahvins?'

'Yes.'

'To do us harm.'

'No, no,' she answered quickly, fearing unpleasant repercussions. 'The Drahvins are holding a friend of ours prisoner. We had to do as they told us.'

'And what was that?'

Vicki had not been harmed so far, so she stuck to the truth, though with some reluctance. 'To help them capture your spaceship.'

'Why do they want to capture it?' the Chumbley asked. 'We have offered to take them with us.'

'They didn't tell us that.'

'No. They would not. They would rather kill. It is regrettable, but they hate us.'

'Well, you did kill one of them.'

89

'We never destroy life deliberately. That is not our way.'

Vicki was aware of a growing bafflement. 'Look,' she said, 'who is this talking? Is it this Chumbley or is it . . . someone else?'

'You call the machines Chumblies?'

'For want of a better name, yes.'

'The Chumblies have a speaker in them,' the voice said. 'They are transmitting our thoughts. We do not speak as you do, because we have no vocal chords. We communicate telepathically. It is difficult to convert thought-waves into sound language, but our scientists finally mastered the art.'

She was feeling more at ease now. The statement that they never destroyed life deliberately had been a comfort to her. She had little choice but to believe them. She crouched and peered into the Chumbley's visor. 'But who are you?'

'We are the Rills.'

She turned her gaze back to the eyes at the viewport. 'That's you, is it?'

'Correct.'

'Then why do you stay in there? Why not come out, so that I can see you?'

Again the eyes leisurely closed and opened again. 'It is better that you do not see us. Not all the dominant species in the universe look like men. Our appearance might shock you as it did the Drahvins. It would not be the first time that has happened to us. It will not be the last.'

His hands well inside the grill now, the Doctor was

investigating the top plates of the air converter. He hummed tunelessly to himself as his fingers moved lightly over them and found more screws. Yes, he would be able to get the plates off in no time, then proceed with rendering it inoperable. It was his firm intention to do that not only to the converter, but the Rills as well. No step was too long if it meant getting Vicki out.

He moved his screwdriver in.

Vicki was puzzled. She was confronted with an anomaly and it irritated her. 'You claim you never deliberately destroy life, but the Drahvin leader says you attacked them. Which is true?'

'That certainly is not. We were investigating space above this planet when we encountered a ship of a type we had never seen before. Rills do not attack or kill without compelling reason, so we stopped our ship and waited. They also stopped. We hung in space facing each other, this planet turning beneath us and the suns above. We would have turned and left, but that would have made us vulnerable and we feared attack. We did all we could to transmit messages of peace, both by thought and by space-waves – we even tried radio – but no response came. We had to conclude that either they did not use such systems or they meant us harm, in which case we were best advised to stay where we were. So we hung there for four dawns and finally decided to take the risk and leave. As we were turning the Drahvins opened fire, hitting us on the side. To preserve ourselves, we returned the fire and were successful, rather more than they were because our armament turned out to be superior to theirs. Both of us managed to make a landing on this planet.

'When we escaped from our ailing ship we found that we could not breathe the atmosphere here, but we had a small portable supply of our own and set out to see if we could help the Drahvins. We should not have taken the trouble.

'The first one we found was badly injured, so we started to help her. We had taken medication with us and considered that we could save her life. This was our intention, but it was not to be.'

The Rill paused and considered: 'You must understand that when I said it was best that you did not see us it was because we have learnt that our appearance, normal to us, is revolting to other species. We have heads, we are scaled and we have tentacles, six of which have hands much like yours and without which we could not have reached our present level of evolution. But we are ugly, perhaps sinister, certainly horrific in the eyes of others. This is a pity, because our appearance provokes revulsion and aggression. That is why we normally remain concealed when visiting other planets, at least until we know we are not going to be set upon.

'We can understand Maaga's reaction when she saw creatures such as us doing she knew not what to her soldier, with our machines busily helping, but we find it difficult to excuse the fact that she immediately raised her gun and opened fire on us. One of us was seriously injured before the machines could raise the force-shield about us, so we gathered him up and set off back to here.'

Vicki was absorbed in the picture his words had painted. 'But why didn't you shoot back?'

'We could have done. Our weapons are superior to theirs. But our force-shield was sufficient protection and, as I said, we do not kill. The Drahvins do.

'When we looked back we saw Maaga standing over the injured soldier. She pointed her gun down and killed her. It was a sad and brutal sight to see.'

Vicki was appalled. 'But all the Drahvins believe you did it.'

'We know. That is why they keep attacking us.'

'And would you really have taken them off with you in your ship?'

'Why not? We could have arranged accommodation with air for them. What do we gain if they die? We found a way to convey this to the woman Maaga, but all she does is to curse us, to bury us in hate and to bury us physically if she can, though I doubt if she would honour us with such a dignity.' The Rill had noticed Vicki shifting restlessly from one foot to another. 'Something is worrying you.'

'I wish I could see the whole of you,' Vicki admitted.

'It is better that you don't. Besides, we cannot come out. In order to live we must have ammoniac gas. That is the atmosphere of our home planet. So we live here in a compartment where it is filtered in.'

Vicki was horrified. 'You can't breathe oxygen at all?'

'No. We would die immediately.'

Vicki gasped, turned and tried to make for the passageway from which she had recently entered. But the Chumbley balked her, dodging this way and that whichever way she tried to get round it. 'For Heavens' sake!' she finally screamed. 'Let me out, or you'll all be killed!'

'Killed? By whom?'

'The Doctor. My friend.' She was wild-eyed with panic. 'He's wrecking your converting machine! You're all going to die!'

The Doctor knew better than to hurry things. When confronted with circuits as complicated as these, despite their relatively simple purpose, calmness was the order of the day. Haste would only produce delay. 'Gently, gently,' he murmured to himself, delicately lifting out yet another part of the circuitry and dropping it into the various items he had already removed.

In went his hands again. It would not take long now.

Steven still feigned sleep, breathing deeply and regularly, but slowly opening his eyelids a fraction to look at his guard. He sighed inwardly as he saw that his hopes had been realised. She was nodding with sleep over her gun. All was quiet, not a sound or movement to be detected. The poor thing had had a long day. If he had anything to do with it, it was going to turn out rather longer than she anticipated. Taking great care not to make the slightest noise which might awaken her, he raised himself to a sitting position. Having achieved that, he raised his legs and turned so that he could stand. There was a tiny squeak from the material beneath him. The Drahvin's head jerked a little and she mumbled something indistinguishable, then it nodded again and she returned to her dreams of death.

Now he was sitting directly in front of her, holding his breath and praying that this was going to work. He raised his hands, one aimed at her mouth, the other at her gun. Then he lunged forward and kept going. The chair went over backwards, but the gun was in his grasp and pointing threateningly at the disarmed woman. There was no need for it, however. Her head had thudded against the deck when she fell. She groaned and rolled over, unconscious.

Steven crouched and examined her briefly. There was no sign of blood and he could hear her breathing, almost snoring, so he straightened and listened. The chair had clattered a little as it went over, but all else remained silent. Satisfied that all was well for the moment, he trod gently to the lever set in the bulkhead and pressed it down. The door began to hum open, when he heard Maaga's voice from behind him. 'Quick, he is escaping.'

Steven rushed into the airlock, intending to escape through the outer door, but it was sealed. To the side he saw two buttons and promptly hit the top one. The door behind him hummed shut and he turned to see a furious Maaga staring through the window at him. Her harsh voice came to him from a speaker above his head. 'You cannot escape. Give up and we will not harm you.'

'I'd be a fool to believe that, wouldn't I?' he replied.

'Give up!'

'Drop dead!'

He saw her hand reaching for the opening lever and his mind raced. The airlock was sealable so that a person could leave without anything from a hostile environment leaking into the main body of the ship. It therefore followed that if the outer door was open there was no way in which the inner could be at the same time. It was worth a try. He stabbed the lower button. The outer door slid open and he heard Maaga shout, 'The machines will kill you!' Her voice had a hint of hysteria in it.

But that concerned him not at all. Holding the gun before him, he stepped out into the half-light that this planet knew as night, the three suns being too widely spaced to permit real darkness. Pausing a moment, he breathed deeply of air that was fresher than that of the ship, then set off in the direction Vicki and the Doctor had taken.

However, he took only a few steps and halted. A Chumbley was moving toward him and looking to him as though it meant business. He stared at it in disbelief. How many of them could there be? They were everywhere. And worst of all, one of them was here, just at the wrong moment.

He stood briefly in indecision, then, seeing nothing else for it, dived reluctantly back into the airlock and pressed the bottom button. Through the viewport he saw the Chumbley come to a halt. It stayed there, clearly with no intention of going until something further developed. His escape route was blocked. He turned hopelessly toward the inner compartment of the ship.

Maaga was watching him. The smile on her face held more threat than humour.

Air was still being drawn into the vent, but the Doctor knew he had reached the heart of it. He was beginning to understand how ingenious a piece of technology it was. There were so many failsafe devices in it that no sooner had he cut one out than another took its place. But now there was only one left. Very delicately he poised the screwdriver above it and almost jumped out of his skin as Vicki's voice screamed from behind him, 'No, Doctor, no!'

It took him several seconds to collect himself. 'Bless my soul, girl, try not to do that when I'm concentrating, will you? It does my heart no good at all.'

'I was afraid I'd be too late.'

He turned and saw her looking through the grill, a Chumbley close behind her. 'Too late for what?'

The bars slid up before her and she stepped out into the half-light by which the Doctor had been working. 'The Rills won't harm us. They want to help.'

The Chumbley moved up beside her. 'We were told your friend is in danger.'

The Doctor glanced nervously about him. 'Who said that?'

'This did,' Vicki answered, resting a maternal hand on the machine's head.

'Ah, did it?' The Doctor peered at it. 'I take it that is a Rill talking?'

'If you care to put it that way, yes. You'd better answer him.'

The Doctor addressed the Chumbley, feeling something of a fool for doing so. 'You were told correctly. Our friend is in serious trouble.'

'Then perhaps you will both come inside.'

The Doctor hesitated. 'It occurs to me that if we do that we could both be trapped.'

'Doctor,' Vicki said, 'if they meant us any harm this Chumbley could shoot us now.'

'Yes, yes,' he nodded in agreement. 'Quite true. Very well, lead the way.'

The Chumbley pivoted and made for the entrance. Before it reached it, however, one of its brothers came scudding out and chumbled off into the distance. The Doctor looked after it. 'Where's he going in such a hurry?'

'To repair the damage you and your friend did to its fellow machine. We are sending another to do the same for the converter.'

'Ah.' The Doctor looked suitably apologetic, then grimaced at Vicki.

They followed the Chumbley along the passageway and into the main chamber, the machine circling to a halt. The Doctor looked about him with as much interest as he had the first time, then a thought occurred to him. He rapped his cane smartly on the Chumbley's head. 'What are you drilling for, may I ask?'

'Power. We need a great deal in order to launch our vessel and the suns are too weak to supply it. Therefore, by drilling we hope to find some beneath us.'

'Then if you take my advice,' the Doctor said,

'you'll find it quickly. You don't have much time.'

The guard on the viewport slid up and the great eyes surveyed them again. 'You know about the explosion of this planet?'

'Rather more than you do. It's nearly dawn now. There's only one to go and that's the end.'

There came a pause while the Rill absorbed this new information. 'Then we have no chance of survival.'

'But you've finished repairing the ship?' Vicki asked.

'Yes. But the only fuel we can find is gas and that is of no use to us. We have no means of converting it into the solar power we need.'

'Solar,' the Doctor mused. 'Meaning nuclear. You're going to help us and I think we can help you. I can supply the power you need.'

'We would be deeply grateful.'

'And that's another thing,' Vicki said. 'You keep saying "we". How many of you are there?'

'Four.'

'That doesn't seem many for manning a ship like yours.'

'We were twelve. Seven of us died in the crash and one has been seriously wounded by Maaga. He is not able to carry out his duties.'

The Doctor nodded sympathetically, then became businesslike. 'I shall require some metal-cored cable.'

'We have some.'

'Good. We should be able to effect a transference from our ship to this. I just hope your cable will take it, because we don't have much time and I'll have to flood it through. You'll have to do a little conversion this end first. Can you manage that?'

'We shall do all you say. You are our only—'

The voice stopped abruptly and the Chumbley chittered to itself. There came a whirring sound from the Rills' chamber and a clicking as from a control panel.

'What's the matter?' the Doctor queried. 'What's happening?'

'We have just received a message from one of our machines,' the Rill said. 'It is posted by the Drahvin spaceship. It reports that a being, not Drahvin, came out of it and assumes it was your friend. But before contact could be made he went back in again.'

'That's Steven,' Vicki cried. 'He still thinks you're dangerous.'

'We shall go and talk to him.'

The Doctor was firm. 'Not yet you won't. First things first, which in this case happens to be the transference of power. We'll have the cable. Steven can look after himself for the moment.'

Maaga's smile was almost a leer as she looked in upon Steven. So much for the machinations of this particular male who thought he could tangle with her. Despite his clever talk he possessed only the mentality of a slave, which was minimal. He was about to learn that it was unwise to challenge the Drahvin élite, a lesson he would never forget, unless something terminal happened to shorten the memory.

'If you throw your gun down I will open the airlock,' she said and saw him tighten his grip on the gun, an expression of anger coming over his face. It made little difference to her. She had encountered the odd slave in revolt before. Invariably the revolution had been short-lived and often bloody in its conclusion. 'Very well. But if you try to come through here, you may possibly kill one or two of my soldiers, but you will go as well.' She saw him look over his shoulder. 'Yes, outside the machine awaits you. You would appear to have painted yourself into a corner.'

'So I stay here,' Steven replied. 'I may be trapped, but you can't harm me.'

'Indeed? Then let me give you some information. On the bulkhead beside you there are some dials. They are pressure gauges.'

She saw his glance at them. 'What of it?'

She poised herself for the telling thrust, enjoying herself now, all anger gone, to be replaced by undiluted pleasure at the suffering about to befall him. 'We can draw the oxygen out of that section. You are about to suffocate.' As Steven turned to look out of the port and began to raise a hand to the button, she continued, 'I don't think I would do that if I were you, because if you do you will then be completely at the mercy of the machine and that would be a pity. Look at it this way: if you stay where you are you at least have a tiny chance of survival. I know it is only *very* tiny, but there we are, we have to live with these problems thrown up from time to time – if "live" is the word. Whereas if you open the outer door your end is certain.'

The expression of bafflement on his face was a

pleasure for her to see. She signalled to her soldiers and Drahvins Two and Three moved the panel and grasped a control wheel each.

'Ready,' said Drahvin Two.

Maaga nodded. 'Pressure?'

'Normal.'

'Temperature?'

'Normal.'

'Good. Empty airlock – and do it slowly.'

This was all very pleasing. It was not often she had the chance of such sport. She had really boxed this one in, leaving him three options. He could die in the airlock, come in and die at her hands, or go out and be killed by the machine. This promised to be a fun day.

Vicki and the Doctor were sorting through roll upon roll of cable suspended from the deckhead. All of them were light in weight, but the Doctor had examined their cores and could see that, though fine, almost thread-like, they were capable of carrying considerable power. They would need to be for what he had in mind. He held one up so that the Rill could see it. 'Would this do it? Please bear in mind that there's going to be a tremendous surge and I don't want anything burning out. We don't have the time to go through all this again.'

'Then you had better take the one second along on your left. That is our strongest.'

The Doctor moved to it and ran out a length. There was no point in his examining it because he was not familiar with their technology. He would have liked to have been, but this was neither the time nor the place.

Perhaps another day, if he was lucky. He was warming to the Rills, indifferent to their physical appearance, but moved by their sensibility. In his experience, time and space were heavily over-populated with villains. What was called for was a serious culling to thin them out and give species like the Rills a better chance. Devil take the main-chancers who cheated at every opportunity and too often ended up winning because of the power their treachery brought them.

These thoughts occupied him as, with Vicki's assistance, he took the cable as far as the entrance to the passageway. There he stopped and addressed the Chumbley beside them. 'We're a fair distance away. Is this going to be long enough?'

'I was wondering that,' Vicki said.

'It will be adequate,' came from the machine. 'We try to allow for all foreseeable emergencies.'

'Good. Then we'll be on our way.'

At that moment there was more noise from the Rills' control boards. All paused and waited until it ceased.

'What was that?' Vicki asked.

There was a pause, then the Rill answered. 'The machine on guard at the Drahvin ship has reported that your friend is still inside. But he is making noises that it cannot understand. It says they sound like cries of distress. He has relayed them to me and I think the same. Your friend is in need of assistance.'

'Then we'd better give it,' the Doctor snapped.

'You cannot help him alone,' the Rill said. 'We shall send two of the machines with you.'

'What can they do?' a worried Vicki demanded.

'If necessary, they can cut the ship wide open.'

'We might need it,' the Doctor said, hurrying into the passageway. 'Come on, Vicki. Quickly!'

They burst out into the open and the two Chumblies came chittering along on their heels. Then the machines gathered speed and alternated between leading the way and circling about like guards, chumbling over the rough terrain as though it did not exist and chittering excitedly to themselves as they remained in contact with the Rills. Both Vicki and the Doctor were thankful for their presence as they raced for the Drahvins' ship, both knowing that without such support they would never be able to come to the assistance of Steven. It was good to have them along in such a time of crisis.

The two came to a sudden and panting halt as they were confronted by Drahvin Three, who rose from behind some of the planet's flora, her gun aimed at them. The Chumblies also stopped, but the Doctor could hear them still relaying information to the Rills.

'Where are you going?' the Drahvin said.

'Back to your spaceship, of course,' the Doctor gasped. 'Surely even you can see that?'

'Why do you bring the machines with you? They are our enemies.'

'They are not,' the Doctor insisted. 'They're here to help you and Maaga get to their spaceship so that you'll be safe.'

She remained stony. 'Maaga does not trust you. I do not trust you.'

Oh, what a cretin, the Doctor thought, Steven's

plight uppermost in his mind. 'Look,' he said, 'these machines do as we tell them. Watch.' He turned to the Chumblies and prayed that the Rills could hear him through them. 'Go forward.'

They did so until he cried, 'Stop!' They did that too. The Doctor sighed with relief.

'Come back,' he said and they returned to him, as docile as well-trained dogs. The Doctor gave the Drahvin what he hoped was a winning smile. 'There, you see. Now we'll be on our way.'

'I am going to kill you,' the Drahvin said.

But she never managed it because the moment she had uttered the words a beam lanced out from one of the Chumblies and enveloped her weapon. She cried out in pain and the beam immediately vanished. To her complete consternation she found herself holding nothing but a handgrip. She dropped it, lowered her hands and looked at them with eyes blank of understanding. 'You had better kill me. I have failed in my duty.'

'Oh, don't be silly,' Vicki snapped impatiently.

The Doctor felt the same way. 'Silly girl. Now come along with us. That's an order.'

The Drahvin lowered her head in shame, but nonetheless followed as the party resumed its trek toward the spaceship.

Steven's mouth hung slack and gaping as he gasped for air. Sweat beaded his forehead, fell and steadily soaked his shirt. His heart fought to function normally, despite the fact that it was being starved of oxygen, but was losing the battle. It hammered this

105

way and that, like a trapped tiger, and found little to keep itself operational.

The gauge needles eased their way steadily downward.

'Why do you not give up?' Maaga asked, not really wishing him to.

Bereft of speech, his lungs struggling to consume what little remained of the oxygen and sparing nothing for such an unnecessary exercise, Steven stared at her in hatred, feeling his eyes bulging, his head spinning, but still retaining his grip on the gun. He staggered to the release button for the outer door and again Maaga spoke. 'That will do you no good. The doors will not open until the pressure is normal. Why waste your strength? After all, there isn't much of it left, is there?'

Steven fell against the wall and rested his forehead on it, one hand supporting him. But his legs were weakening. He started to slide downward.

4

The Exploding Planet

Maaga could see that the young man had not much
longer to live. His face was purple, his tongue
hanging out. His chest laboured mightily for air, but
there was almost none remaining. He was on his knees
and close to toppling the rest of the way. Then
unconsciousness would come and, soon after, the end
for him. It was a pity to lose a hostage, but he had
given her no alternative. Then, too, the Doctor and
the girl had no way of knowing about Steven's
hastened demise. That they would learn on their
return, by which time it would be too late. Maaga
would have them once again and, if necessary, would
use the girl as a hostage to replace the dead one. It
would all work out in the end, she thought, watching
Steven's final struggle for survival. She would get
herself and her soldiers off this doomed planet and up
into the freedom of outer space, there to resume the
search for a place suitable for colonisation. It could be
inhabited or not. The matter was unimportant to her.
Anyway, a resident population could prove
convenient. After the necessary culling they could be
put to any purpose the élite chose, whether they

resisted or not. Resistance, too, could be a good thing. It speeded the cull.

'Soon he will die,' Drahvin Two said from beside her.

'It was his own doing,' she said briefly.

The Drahvin nodded and continued watching the struggling Steven with eyes as calm as those of a scientist studying a blood slide.

'Machine approaching!' Drahvin Three called.

Maaga went to a port and looked out, to see the accursed thing moving in. This one was carrying a metal sphere in its arms. It looked to be a bomb. What was the point, she wondered. The bombs never seriously harmed her ship and the robots never used their weapons against it. The reason for this totally evaded her, but their every attack was a plentiful waste of time. To keep it up repeatedly was nothing short of an exercise in pointlessness. She did not even feel inclined to order her soldiers to their stations. That was equally as futile. Anyway, it was possible that they would soon need all the armament they could get. A skirmish with the Rills was inevitable. She would conserve all the power possible.

The Chumbley approached the side of the ship and set the bomb against it. That done, it moved away, but only a short distance this time. As soon as it stopped the bomb went off, shaking the ship hardly at all. Maaga was puzzled. Why such a trivial explosion? Could it be that the Rills were running out of supplies? If so, such a state of affairs could only be to her benefit.

The explosion, however, had also penetrated the clouds of Steven's drifting mind. He opened his eyes and with one last supreme effort levered himself up to the viewport. As soon as it detected his movement the Chumbley swung its head from side to side. Steven could not make out why it was doing so. He could not know that the machine was trying to tell him to stand aside. Nor did he any longer have the wit to do so, until it sent a brief stab of laser at the bottom of the port. The smoke and flame sent him crashing to the deck, almost certainly never to rise again.

Once he had done so, the Chumbley notched its weapon up to three-quarter power and loosed off a bolt at the side of the door, this time cutting straight through. Air screamed in, but the machine did not pause. It moved the ray steadily round until the door fell completely away. Steven could not believe it. He gulped savagely at the sweet air, so savagely indeed that he hurt his lungs in the process. He got to his feet, swayed and fell through the door to the ground. He looked up and flinched as he saw the Chumbley standing over him. He was even more shaken when he heard it say, 'Please be calm. You are safe now and your friends are on their way.'

'Is that you talking?' he asked in bafflement.

'The machine you see before you is relaying my voice. We are the Rill.'

Steven put his hands on the Chumbley and raised himself to his feet. 'I take it I'm a prisoner, then.'

'You are not. The Doctor explained your predicament to us and we have freed you, as you see.'

Steven looked back at the warped door lying on the ground and the scorched and blackened space from which it had come. 'You did quite a job.'

'We try to help.'

He was recovering from his ordeal now. 'I think I owe you a vote of thanks.'

'You are quite welcome. Are your friends not there yet?'

Steven looked up and saw Vicki and the Doctor hurrying toward him, their escort swirling about them as though indulging in some peculiar waltz. 'They're just arriving.'

Vicki rushed up to him and embraced him. 'Oh, Steven, are you all right?'

'I am now,' he said, patting the Chumbley's head. 'Thanks to this little fellow who, I might say, packs quite a punch.'

The Doctor hauled up alongside them, as out of breath as was usual of late. He glanced at Steven to make sure the lad was all right, then turned his gaze on the Drahvin ship. 'Our friend Maaga isn't going to be too pleased about this,' he observed.

He was right. Maaga's face was black with frustration and fury as she stood before her three soldiers. 'Guns ready,' she snapped bleakly.

The three brought up their guns and set their switches in readiness.

'Door.'

Drahvin One turned and depressed the lever. The door hummed open.

'After them and kill!'

They hurried out through the door and the airlock into the open air, to halt abruptly as they saw the three Chumblies pointing their guns at them. They made to lift theirs and aim, but the leading Chumbley, visor flashing, spoke. 'Do not attempt to fire upon us or we shall do the same, rather more quickly than you. Do not mistake our intention. It is to kill if you attempt to interfere.'

The Drahvins lowered their weapons and stood quite still at a muttered order from Maaga. She stared at her enemies in total hatred, unable to believe that she had been thwarted by such an ill-assorted trio of humans, particularly that ridiculous-looking Doctor, like something which had slothfully emerged from between the dried pages of time and would be well-advised to return there. Had it not been for the machines she would have had him and put an end to his machinations in short order. But her chance would come. Of that she was sure.

'Doctor, please bring your party away,' one of the Chumblies said.

The Doctor jerked away from contemplation of the expression on Maaga's face. He did not think he had ever seen such loathing in his life, though it was all of a piece with her attitude toward life. 'Certainly.' He turned to Steven. 'Can you walk, young man?'

Steven nodded. 'I'll be all right.'

'Come along then.'

Without sparing another glance for the Drahvins, they set off behind the Chumbley, another one bringing up the rear. Steven was still short of breath, but inhaled deeply of the sweet and precious air. It was not something that he had ever bothered to appreciate before. After all, it had always been there and taken for granted. Now that he had been without it for a time things would never be that way again. Whenever and wherever he was in time and space his appreciation of it would be alive and well and living in his lungs.

The remaining Chumbley addressed Maaga. 'You will take your soldiers back into the ship and you will stay there.'

Maaga gave it a savage look.

'Until now we have spared you,' it continued, 'even though you have attacked us repeatedly. Now our patience is at an end and we have determined to deal severely with any further attempts on your part. Heed our warning and heed it well. It is you who will pay the consequences of any breach of this ruling. We shall protect both ourselves and our friends.'

'Friends!' Maaga sneered.

The Chumbley ignored her. 'Go back inside and do not attempt to leave.'

'But the air is disgusting in there,' Maaga protested. 'Your bomb has made it almost unbreathable.'

'It will have cleared by now. The ammonia bomb was only a warning. Go inside.'

'Come,' Maaga said and the three Drahvins followed her inside. Once in the cabin Maaga looked out through the port. The Chumbley was still there and making no movement. Only the light glowed in its visor. She thought disgustedly that the infernal thing looked as though it might eventually take root. Though not before she did it a serious mischief, she mentally added.

'Is it still there, Maaga?' Drahvin Two asked.

'It is.'

'Then we cannot escape to destroy the Rills and the others.'

'We cannot escape *yet*,' Maaga corrected her. 'But we will. No Drahvin is defeated until dead. Is that correct?'

'Yes, Maaga,' all three intoned.

'Remember it,' she said, then turned to Drahvin Three. 'Does the forward hatch still operate?'

'Yes, Maaga,' Three replied.

'Silently?'

'Yes.'

An idea began to crystallise in her mind. It was not much, but in such a situation as theirs any action was better than none. 'Soon now it will be dimlight. Then it will be night, the last one this planet will know. We must capture the Rill vessel before dawn. When I tell you to, you will leave through the hatch. You will then circle round behind the machine. Understood?'

'Yes, Maaga,' Three answered obediently, no shadow of misgiving entering her iron mind.

'And you will destroy it. Then we shall be free to put paid to the others.'

Steven did not like the all-pervading smell of ammonia in the main Rill chamber. It pricked at his nostrils and brought tears to his eyes. But Vicki had forewarned him; he knew it was the life-source of the Rills.

Not that he was inclined to be critical. He owed his life to the Rills and their powerful little machines. Now it just seemed plain foolish to him that they had run from the Chumblies and even disabled one. How blind can man be, he wondered. Where does his lack of understanding end, or is he doomed to stumble endlessly on into eternity? But at least there was the

113

ability to learn and adapt. Already he was beginning to accept even the huge liquid eye steadily and languidly observing them through the viewport, though the leisure of its blinking still fascinated him. The Rill seemed to have all the time in the world, no need of haste, possessed only of tranquillity.

Vicki was watching the Doctor examining the end of the cable. He was lost in thought. 'There can't be much time left, Doctor,' she warned.

'I'm aware of that,' he said absently. 'But it's no good doing a transfer as powerful as I intend if all I achieve is to blow the cable. Anyway, we have about ten or twelve hours before wipe-out.'

'Not so, Doctor,' came from the Chumbley beside him. 'Only some six hours remain.'

The Doctor cocked his head. 'Surely not.'

'Only one of the three suns is constant. That is the leading one. The others are rogue suns, their orbits erratic. This is the period when they depart from the main one and pursue their own courses and normally would return within three dawns. However, things will not be normal. Six hours remain to us.'

Vicki and Steven were appalled, but the Doctor remained calm. It was not in his nature to succumb to panic. For the time being his concern was to make a transfer of powr from the TARDIS to the Rill vessel. That he intended to do. He could only trust in Fate that the cable would withstand the force of it.

'It will take much time to make the transfer,' the Rill said.

'Then we'll have to be quick, won't we?'

'We are concerned for your safety.'

114

'Yes, yes, very noble, but we also are concerned for yours.' He held out the cable to the Chumbley. 'Haul that along, will you? We're wasting time in this idle gossip.'

The Chumbley paused, then took it.

'D'you want me with you, Doctor?' Steven asked.

'No. You stay here and let us know immediately if anything goes wrong. I'll take Vicki.'

'OK.'

The Doctor bustled outside, Vicki and the Chumbley with him. Steven watched them go, then squeezed his nose in an attempt to stop the irritation from the ammoniac gas. It achieved very little. He wiped away the recently-formed tears and looked about him. There's no place like home, he thought as he viewed the functionalism of everything and tried in vain to detect the source of the light illuminating the area. He still could not fully accept the benign nature of the Rills. Not normally given to mistrust, he was rapidly learning to use it as a defence mechanism since the Doctor had invaded his life. 'So the Doctor trusts you?' he idly asked the air in general, not yet having fully adjusted to talking to machines.

'Should he not?'

'I don't know, do I? I'm sure you produced the right ethical reasons for him, so naturally he would.'

'But not you?'

'I reserve my opinion.'

'Despite the fact that our machines rescued you from the Drahvins.'

'For all I know, you might be just the same as they are – using us for your own salvation.'

115

'That is not the case.'

'That's very easy to say,' Steven persisted. 'But just suppose that something went wrong and the Doctor couldn't manage to charge your ship up in time. After all, there's plenty of room for error. The question then arises: would you hold us here or would you let us vanish in our own ship, the TARDIS?'

'It only becomes a question if your mind is full of doubt.'

'Mine is, and I admit it,' Steven said. 'I can't see you letting us go, just like that.'

'Then I am sorry. We are strange beings to you. You have probably never met anything like us. But do not permit appearances to cloud your judgement. We mean you well. I understand your difficulty, of course. You come from Earth, a planet we do not know, but clearly it is one which still knows conflict.'

Steven had to ruefully accept the observation, as he recalled that at any given moment on Earth there was at least one war going on somewhere. There was hatred, murder and horror aplenty, little enough to be proud of but sufficient to compel human beings to proceed through life with caution, even mistrust. He wished he could accept the altruism of the Rills as readily as the Doctor obviously had, but his conditioning was too strong and, anyway, it had stood him in good stead thus far in his life. There was no good reason to discard it, particularly since the Doctor had this gift for landing them in one scrape after another.

What he did not know was that the Rill was as much lost in thought as he was, wondering why the human form, or something like it, was so prevalent in the universe: two legs, two arms leading to hands with the vital opposing thumbs and a brain. The origins were too far back in time to be traced, yet there seemed little of genuine advantage in it. There was much more to be said for that of the 'Rills, sufficient tentacles and enough hands, though it had to be admitted that the head enclosing the brain was somewhat cumbersome, the skull far thicker than was necessary. Yet it had afforded protection in the darker days when there had been predatory species on their planet and without it there would probably be no Rills surviving. The skull could be thinned, of course, but the process was tiresome and there was no real need for it. The females of his species favoured it more than their counterparts, but there was little point. Anyone who happened to be passing could and did fertilise an egg. The presence of a particular male was not essential, though more often than not the females tried to make it seem so.

To a certain extent he envied mankind that easily-carried skull, yet there was always a drawback. They moved and lived too quickly and thus rendered their lives too short, though he was not too sure about the Doctor person. Something about him cried out a vast experience of life, though how he had acquired it was a mystery to be pondered upon when time was of less importance, when they were safely home and moving in their normal way, some fifty times more slowly than the humans. Thought, too, could be adjusted to whatever speed was required, though twice the speed of their movements made the Rills most comfortable.

Thinking at human speed was wearing, as was the mere observation of their rapid motion. It was in no way surprising that they wore out their bodies in such a short space of time. Perhaps eventually they would learn the true value of conserving energy, rather than needlessly expending it in unnecessary effort, though he thought possibly not. Perhaps without the expenditure something went wrong with their bodies. He did not know.

But they thought well enough, he had noted, and their social order was clear and conscientiously observed. The Doctor had been quick to find an answer to their power deficiency and the other two constantly deferred to him, though without surrendering their individuality. He was their leader, their superior. Much the same order prevailed on his home planet, but since there was so little activity it was seldom called for. Thought was their pleasure, sometimes on corporeal matters, more often on the abstract. What need was there for physical exertion when a gentle stretching of the mind served as well or indeed better? Anyway, it was simple enough to design machines capable of tending to the more mundane tasks. What was it the girl had called them? Chumblies? He converted it into a thought pattern and found it pleasing. He must communicate it to his fellow Rills as soon as the opportunity offered. They would be interested and might even find it as amusing as he did.

The human being was restless, fidgeting here and there about the chamber. He looked up at the Rill. 'There's something you should know.'

'What is that?'

'While I was in the Drahvins' ship they said they were determined to leave in yours.'

'We are prepared to take them with us.'

'That's not what they meant. They want to take your ship and leave you here.'

'We must hope they do not succeed.'

'With time running out they'll be desperate. You'd better let me fix the Doctor's cable at this end.'

'Thank you. I will inform the Doctor of what you are doing. One of the machines will help you. It will be quicker.'

Steven made for the cable. 'It'll need to be.'

Drahvin Three crawled on all fours to the escape hatch, Maaga behind her. Once there, she grasped the locking wheel and strained to open it. At first it looked as though it was going to refuse to budge, but finally it broke free and she was able to spin it. She eased the hatch down and open. 'I am ready, Maaga.'

'Then go.' Maaga reached forward and placed a thick metal bar in her waiting hand. 'And do not fail.'

'I shall not,' Three said and wriggled through the hatch and along the short entry tunnel. The bar clinked once, but otherwise she moved in almost complete silence, to drop gently to the ground outside.

It was dusk now, but she knew that complete darkness never fell because the two rogue suns, shooting off into their own orbits, were never so far away as to leave the planet in blackness. She heard Maaga closing the hatch door behind her and turning

119

the wheel only twice to barely hold it shut. She struck off to the side, away from the ship and, more importantly, away from the Chumbley guarding it. The going was not too difficult, but she had to keep a sharp eye out for the unexpected cracks in the surface. Her dainty feed trod light and her delicate hand firmly clasped the murderous-looking metal bar.

Behind her, Maaga turned away from the viewport and spoke to the two remaining soldiers seated dumbly at the table. 'I cannot see her any more.'

'She will die willingly,' Drahvin One said.

'She will not die until she eliminates that machine,' Maaga snapped.

'And shall we escape, Maaga?' Drahvin Two wanted to know.

'Once the robot is gone, yes.'

There was a dangerous rumbling. The ship began to tremble about them. It grew to a roar, then slowly faded, but not completely. It tingled somewhere and spiked the air with a menace that Maaga could feel physically. Her face was grim.

Drahvin Two turned her empty face to her leader. 'What is happening?'

'It's the first warning of the explosion to come,' she replied. 'There are only hours left. Soldier Three must work quickly.'

Drahvin Three could see the guardian Chumbley clearly now. It had not moved so much as a fraction, but she knew that caution was called for and bore its warning well to the fore of her mind. If it once detected her she was as good as dead. That in no way disturbed her; it was an honour to die in battle. What did was that she would be wasted and Maaga disappointed. She could not allow that to happen. Hardly daring to breathe, she slipped forward, a lovely killer flitting through the half-light of a foreign planet. She was almost upon the machine when she stopped. For no apparent reason the Chumbley tweeted quietly to itself, then fell silent again.

She stole forward and found herself directly behind it. Hefting the bar in two hands, she raised it high above her head, reared up as far as she could, made sure that there was no possibility of missing, and brought the bar smashing down onto the Chumbley's head.

The Doctor and Vicki reached the Rills' outbuilding and went straight inside, a Chumbley with them. Wordlessly the Doctor crossed to where Steven had affixed the cable where the Rills had instructed him. It was surrounded with other terminals. The Doctor could only assume that the Rills knew what they were about. 'I've got the TARDIS end on a time switch,' he said, taking his fob-watch from his pocket and studying it. 'You've got one minute from . . . now.'

'We do not know your measure of time. We await your instruction.'

The Doctor dipped his head and watched the seconds nudge away. All were tense. A Chumbley moved to the panel and extended a claw out to a heavy lever. It waited. The Doctor allowed five reserve seconds to pass beyond the minute, then said, 'Go,' and watched the panel.

'Starting control,' the Chumbley said and pulled the

lever down. An ear-splitting scream filled the air as power from the TARDIS burst through the cable and into the ship's power centre. Vicki and Steven clapped their hands over their ears, but the Doctor was too occupied watching the panel to even notice. As the sound died away he sighed with relief to see that nothing had burnt out.

'Full intake,' the Chumbley said. 'Damage nil. You are to be congratulated, Doctor.'

'So are you, on the strength of your cable,' the Doctor replied. 'Three or four hours should do it. Kindly let me know when you're fully charged.'

'But the planet's going to explode in less than five hours,' Steven protested. 'You're cutting it a bit fine, aren't you?'

The Doctor gave him a beady look. 'Would you have me abandon our friends who, I would remind you, recently saved your life? A little more forethought, young man, before you hurl yourself bodily into a panic. Others are not as tolerant as I am.'

'Quite,' Vicki agreed without hesitation, feeling protective toward both the Rills and the Chumblies.

Steven looked suitably ashamed, as he deserved to. 'I'm sorry,' he mumbled. 'I didn't mean to—'

But he was interrupted by the sounds they knew by now to herald an urgent message coming in from one of the Chumblies. It ceased.

'The Drahvins have escaped and destroyed the machine we left on watch at their ship,' the Chumbley nearby said.

Vicki gasped. 'Oh, no.'

'What about the one outside the TARDIS?' The Doctor demanded.

'We have positioned him safely. He will come to no harm. Meanwhile we shall take steps to intercept the Drahvins. Please continue with the transfer, Doctor.'

'There's nothing to do now but wait.'

'I wish there were,' Steven said. 'This sort of situation makes me restless.'

'Stand still and think of your mother,' Vicki suggested.

Steven gave her a withering smile. 'What a great idea. Did anyone ever tell you you have a marvellous sense of humour?'

'Several people,' she answered brightly.

'They lied.'

Several Chumblies emerged from a doorway, bustled this way and that about the trio, then streamed out through the exit. 'What was all that about?' the Doctor asked the eye still visible through the window.

'They are going to repel the Drahvins, should they attempt to attack the ship. Do not concern yourself about them. They are on full alert now. We would be most surprised if anyone should succeed in catching them unawares.'

'I'm more worried about the cable,' the Doctor said. 'If they cut that you're finished.'

'Have no fear. It is well guarded.'

'It had better be, because if they use the wrong instrument for severing it they'll be blown to eternity.'

'On just a one-way ticket,' Steven added, knowing that the Doctor was not given to exaggeration in matters scientific.

'Calm yourselves,' the voice told them. 'Try to adjust your thought pattern to the time required for waiting.'

Vicki shook her head. 'Maybe you can do that, but we can't. We'd need a course in meditation first.'

'Then I regret I cannot help you.'

Steven thought that a pity. He could have used a little repose right then. The whole thing was becoming too dicey. He was concerned that the Doctor might have bitten off too much this time and could end up in Kingdom Come or wherever it was he had originated. Whatever was to become of Vicki and himself, he had developed a warm affection for the old man and did not want any harm to befall him. Not that there was much he could do. The Doctor knew his own mind and invariably followed it. All that was possible was to watch and wait.

Maaga halted her soldiers on a ridge and lay flat to look down. She could see a Chumbley almost directly below them and others posted at regular intervals, fading into the semi-darkness. There was going to be no easy way to reach the ship, that much was obvious. But she was undeterred. She had fought tougher battles than this promised to be. And probably against worthier opponents, she thought acidly, measuring the strength of the metal patrol and recalling the repulsive sight and smell of their masters. Not only was she a space-Drahvin. Her generalship was considered to be of a high order. She was about to prove it yet again, or willingly die in the attempt. Not for her or her soldiers such a sorry death as to be still on this world when it went nova. That was inconceivable.

She could not immediately see any way of getting one of her soldiers through the screen. The machines would detect her without effort. But there was an alternative. Being only mechanical, as she knew, she suspected that their powers of reasoning were limited, if they existed at all. The question was: how far into them did the Rills exert their control? She had no way of answering that, so was left with no alternative but to act. She turned her head toward Drahvin Two and pointed. 'You go over there and get as close to the third machine as you safely can. Then keep out of detection range and wait.'

'Yes, Maaga.'

'We shall create a diversion to try and draw them away from their positions. The moment you see an opportunity, get through and attack. Do not be diverted by the machines. Our target is the Rill ship. Is that clear?'

'Yes, Maaga.'

'Then go. We shall be with you as soon as we can.'

Drahvin Two backed away from the ridge and made her way in the direction she had been ordered to take. All that occupied what there was of her mind were Maaga's instructions. She would obey them unquestioningly; she was every battle commander's dream, a soldier with no aim other than that which had been drilled into her. She quickly checked the power pack on her gun, then moved on.

Maaga watched her blonde head disappear into the murk, then settled down to wait. She would give her

125

time to get into position before launching her attack. The anticipation would prove trying, but there was nothing else to be done. She glanced at her watch. She would give her soldier ten decilons, Drahvin time, to locate herself and then she would act.

Gun before her, Drahvin Two crouched behind some vegetation and surveyed the Chumbley. It looked a silly machine, but she had experienced its capabilities and knew that caution was called for. Maaga's signal would come soon, then she would take action, which was what she longed for. She wanted more than anything to see people die. She hoped her wish was about to be realised. Knowing Maaga, she thought it highly likely.

The rumbling returned, deep in the bowels of the planet, rising in volume, shuddering the surface as though it were nothing more than the most fragile of tissue paper, turning the sky a dull, threatening orange colour, pressing suffocatingly down on all life forms and seeming to crush the very soil itself. At the peak of its raging, crevices opened up everywhere about the terrain and searing steam screamed up into the sky, to fall back and turn the last night into one of mist and terror. Only reflex action had saved Maaga as she thrust herself away from a jet that sliced its bellowing way upward right beside her. She propelled herself even further from it as she saw the crevice from which it sprang widening itself in her direction like the mouth of a beast gaping for its prey. She knew that the jet was of such a ferocious temperature that it would cut through flesh as though it did not exist and she had no intention of being injured and rendered a burden when their very survival depended upon their taking the Rill ship, no matter what was happening about them. Not that she would long be a burden; the soldiers would kill her without hesitation. They were fighters who travelled light. No excess baggage was allowed to hinder them, not even an injured commander. Through the falling mist she saw their eyes upon her and tightened her grip on her gun.

The sound began to fall away, the jets to drop slowly back. Finally silence fell, but the steam remained, puffing up here and there like passing ghostly trees and pluming the black land with its foggy hint of death to come. Eternity had finished with this place. There was no further use for it.

Maaga raised her gun and sighted at the machine below. 'Stand by.'

The Drahvins also aimed their weapons.

'*Fire*!'

Three beams lanced out at the Chumbley and bathed it in a smouldering glow. They washed up and down the machine, but its visor was closed tight, almost as though it had known what was going to happen. The Drahvins ceased their fire and immediately the visor was up and the gun trained upon them. Barely in time they pressed themselves down as the Chumbley's ray sliced into the ridge and cracked through the air above their heads. Red-hot pieces of rock rained upon them, scorching their clothes and pitting their hands and faces. Their hands furiously beat away the danger.

But the moment the Chumbley paused, Maaga shouted for the Drahvins to spread out and opened fire again. In no time a raging battle was being fought,

127

Maaga and her soldiers firing when they could and constantly shifting position in an attempt to confuse, the Chumbley stabbing away at them with equal regularity. Lasers lashed this way and that, howling through the steamy atmosphere and turning it into a nightmare of destruction.

And Maaga had her wish. In the distance she dimly made out three of the sentries coming to the assistance of the one which stood alone. She smiled in grim satisfaction and loosed off another bolt at the machine below, knowing that all their shots were in vain against it, but equally sure that they were providing the necessary distraction. All was not yet lost.

Drahvin Two watched the Chumbley before her pivot and move away, its multi-coloured lights flashing and its chittering fading as the distance increased. Drahvin Two hefted her weapon and crept toward the Rill centre.

'They sound very close,' Vicki said, tilting her head to the sounds of battle.

'Too close,' Steven added. 'Isn't it possible to charge faster, Doctor?'

The Doctor was absorbed in the dials and gauges before him and the strange markings upon them. 'No, no, utterly impossible. The control panel would be blown out.'

'How do you know?' Steven asked. 'Can you read those dials?'

'Unfortunately, no. I wish I could. But I worked it all out in the TARDIS. That's sufficient for me.'

Vicki was nervous. 'Another earthquake like that

last one and it could be too late for any of this. The ground could open up beneath us.'

But the Doctor was lost again and moved out of sight behind the equipment, trying to interpret the symbols and not succeeding with so hurried a scrutiny. Probably they were not for reading, anyway, since the Rills communicated by thought. They could be mere notchings which triggered impulses to be picked up by the Rill minds. He would probably never find out, more was the pity.

Momentarily separated from the Doctor, Vicki turned to Steven. Her eyes widened and she tapped him on the shoulder. He turned and followed her gaze, to see Drahvin Two standing inside the entry and levelling her gun at them. 'Stand still,' the Drahvin said.

Neither had any intention of moving so much as a finger.

Realising that he could not see his companions, the Doctor made to return to them, only to find himself being buffeted toward a newly-opened entry to the Rills' ship by a determined Chumbley. 'This way, Doctor,' the Rill said. 'Quickly.'

He found himself pushed inside. The door slid to behind him. Ammonia stung his nostrils.

Drahvin Two squinted through her sight at Vicki and Steven. She was about to reach a moment of fulfilment. The knowledge filled her with happy anticipation. 'You escaped once, but you will not do so again.'

Vicki stared in chill horror at the gun-vent from which would leap the laser beam. 'She's going to kill us.'

Steven nodded grimly. 'Then be killed herself.'

'Death does not frighten me,' the Drahvin said. 'I die as a warrior Drahvin and my people will honour me.' Her finger tightened on the trigger. 'Whereas you . . .'

A laser hissed past Steven's shoulder and the Drahvin's mouth jerked open. She stood rigidly, her eyes wider now, but still fastened upon them. Her trigger finger remained fixed. Then she fell and it was no ordinary fall. She went over like a felled tree. Her gun smashed into the floor and bent uselessly to the side. She lay like a graven image, cast in the one mould and doomed never to escape from it.

Vicki and Steven stood in disbelief, until the Chumbley responsible rolled in behind them, chattering away to itself for all the world as though this were an everyday occurrence.

Steven was still stricken with awe at the sight of the statue-like Drahvin lying before them. 'What have you done to her?'

'She is merely paralysed,' the Chumbley said. 'Alive but unconscious.'

'Aren't you going to bring her round again?' Vicki asked.

'We think not. The poor creature does not possess the ability to adjust to life on our planet and we see no reason for her to suffer what will happen at dawn. Better to leave her as she is. Why do you not join the Doctor?'

Steven looked about him. 'Where is he?'

'I'm inside the ship!' the Doctor called. 'Come and see for yourselves!'

Both hesitated. 'Do you think we ought to?' Vicki asked in some trepidation.

'Come along,' the Doctor insisted.

Steven gave Vicki a shrug and they made for the ship's entry, a Chumbley accompanying them.

Maaga and her two remaining Drahvins sat on the ridge, totally exhausted, their guns on the ground beside them. They were soiled and scarred from the flying splinters of soil and rock, their clothes torn and burnt. It had been a mighty struggle, but finally the machines had retreated beneath their fire. It had been just as well, Maaga reflected, because had they stayed much longer her soldiers would have started to fall; she might even have gone down herself. As it was, her left arm was seared from a ray which had come too close. It pained her greatly, but she forced herself to keep their mission well to the front of her mind. They had to take the Rills' ship; the trees of steam were a live reminder of that, if reminder were needed, and she duly awaited the next eruption, not really wondering what it would bring, only if they would be able to survive it. Each one, she knew, would be more severe than the last, on and on in steady progression to the final burst. What they had seen so far was merely the prelude. The full piece would follow ere long. She did not intend to be there when it did.

Had it not been for those machines, she was convinced they could by now have taken the ship and, in the process, destroyed the Rills. But right then she could see no way of defeating them, though there had to be one. Never in her life had she come across an

131

unbeatable foe. She needed time to think. She was not to get it.

Drahvin Three raised her head to listen. 'The machines are returning, Maaga.'

'Again,' Maaga said bitterly and returned to her defence position, noting that her power pack was getting dangerously low. They could not fight for much longer.

The Chumblies came rollicking in across the landscape, chirping and bumbling among themselves and shrugging their way impassively over any obstacles that impeded their path. The only detour they made was to skirt the many steam trees blossoming everywhere. They came to a halt a short distance from where the three Drahvins were concealed and trained their weapons on the spot. Then they fired. Maaga and her soldiers hugged the ground grimly as they prepared to fight out this new assault.

The Rills were sealed off behind a partition of what looked very much like glass or clear perspex. A smoky, greasy gas wreathed them and the Doctor and his companions experienced difficulty in breathing because of the little that had escaped. Vicki and Steven stared hard at what confronted them. No words could convey the reality of what the Rills looked like, but it was enough to make the heart jump and flutter like a trapped bird. The most shocking things to Vicki were the six hands, so human in appearance, yet attached to such monstrous bodies. But she felt no revulsion, perhaps because she had come prepared, but more probably because she now knew how gentle they were beneath their startling exterior. She made herself exhale completely, then inhale only partially in an attempt to calm herself.

'Now you know what we look like,' the Rill said.

'So we do,' the Doctor replied, 'and you, us.'

'We apologise for the glass partition, but you will understand that we must keep our atmosphere in here.'

Adjusting more quickly than Vicki to the sight, Steven found himself puzzled. 'Well, I'm used to you already. So why do the Drahvins hate you so much?'

'We are ugly, so they are frightened. It is a natural reaction, particularly in beings of limited brain-power.'

'Which is them,' Vicki said in annoyance. 'I'll bet you aren't ugly in your own eyes.'

'No, to us our appearance is normal. Yours is not.'

'Only to be expected,' the Doctor said. 'But tell me, don't you move at all – other than your eyelids, that is?'

'We live on a different time-scale to you. To us, your movements are like those of insects, jerking this way and that for no reason at all. When you came into this chamber you came like gusts of wind and as I look at you, you are twitching in a way I would find exhausting. Not even your eyes remain still.'

The Doctor was fascinated. 'How do we compare in relative terms? Do you know our time measures?'

'Now that I know your language, yes. A year to you would be about a week to us. You are burnt out when we are still too young even to learn.'

Not me, the Doctor thought, but my companions, I'm afraid so.

133

'How old are you then?' Steven asked.

'In your terms I am some five hundred years old.'

Vicki was startled into some rapid arithmetic. 'Only ten years old!'

'We are capable of much at that age.'

'I've encountered people who lived such a time-span before,' the Doctor said. 'They arranged it for themselves and as centuries passed they became deeply cynical. There was no joy in their lives. In fact, I could see no purpose at all in their continuing to exist.'

'We passed through that phase,' the Rill observed. 'But that was long ago, though we do have a racial memory of it. It was the younger Rills who noticed, from the example of their elders, that to live for so long with no pleasure and no creativity was futile and was turning life itself into an extended period of waste and bitterness. They it was who slowed us down to our present span and they it was who taught us the exquisite pleasure of possessing time to think and explore. That is why we are here. Ours is a journey taken solely to extend our knowledge and our information banks. It was deeply informative and enjoyable until we encountered the Drahvins.' Then, as an afterthought, he said, 'Yet even they are interesting, as are you. When we have the leisure we shall contemplate the physical similarity between you and them and your totally different psychological structure. That will give us great pleasure.'

'Not all mankind is like us,' Steven said.

'Or even many,' Vicki added.

The Doctor was mildly surprised at her tone.

'Tush, child, Earth is jammed with good people.'

'If you say so.'

He would have to have a talk with her, the Doctor decided. This sort of attitude wouldn't do at all, particularly in one so young and with so much to look forward to. Her life would not add to much measured against eternity, but that was all the more reason to savour every grain of it. Not a speck of life flickered into existence then blacked away that did not, however slightly, determine the course of the life that followed it. Why affect it for the worse? A good talking-to was what she needed and what she would certainly get.

He saw that tears were coursing down her face. 'Are you all right?'

'I feel rather ill,' she choked.

'It must be the ammonia,' Steven said.

The Doctor nodded. 'I should have thought of that.'

'You had better return to the workshop,' the Rill advised. 'Our atmosphere is not good for you.'

'Indeed not,' the Doctor agreed. 'Take the child out, Steven.'

Steven put an arm about Vicki and helped her to the doorway, where she turned and looked back at the Rill. 'I don't suppose we shall see you again.'

'It is improbable.'

'Then goodbye.'

'Goodbye to you, young lady.'

The Doctor bustled out after them, taking his watch out and reading the elapsed time.

Seeing him, Steven asked, 'How much longer have we got?'

'Oh, I should think about an hour,' the Doctor said absently, still preoccupied with what the Rills had said. 'Something like that.'

'Can't you be more definite?'

'What d'you want from me, for Heaven's sake, a countdown?'

Steven clamped his mouth tightly. It was useless talking to the Doctor when he was in this sort of mood. It was his habit to dismiss everything for the sake of the job in hand. In this case it was recharging the Rill ship and what he was dismissing was the Drahvins.

Maaga felt suicidal. Nothing they did affected the machines in the slightest. Their power packs were now nearly empty and they had made no headway at all. A glance at her soldiers confirmed that they too were exhausted and near to dropping, despite their conditioned devotion to duty. There was a limit to everything and they were dangerously close to it. But still the machines kept up an intermittent fire to ensure that they kept their heads down. Time and again their bolts flashed above, so that Maaga wondered if the dreadful things had any power limits at all. It did not seem so. If they did then they did not seem unduly concerned about it, trundling to and fro and loosing off their rays almost with indifference. Perhaps that was the most insulting thing about them to her. Not only were they machines, but they were incapable of caring. She damned the Rills to eternity.

But she had noticed that now all the robots were grouped together, with no regard for their flanks. It could be that the Rills were not sufficiently experienced in fighting to know that, however superior in armament, their machines should be kept well spaced out. Her mind gnawed at the problem as though she were a general pondering his Clausewitz in order to find a way out, which in fact she was.

'We are not defeating them,' Drahvin One said in a drab voice.

'I can see that,' she snapped.

'Perhaps we should attack them with iron bars as Two did,' Drahvin Three suggested.

'You would not get near them before you were gunned down. They are all together, so we shall go round them. If we succeed, make straight for the spaceship. Do not worry about the buildings. We need the ship, so concentrate on that. Come.'

She led them from the ridge, skulking off amid the continuing plumes of steam, their guns still at the ready.

'How much longer?' Steven asked in exasperation.

The Doctor looked over his shoulder from his examination of the gauges. 'Patience, my dear fellow, patience.'

'Dawn is only about half an hour away,' Vicki warned.

Steven grunted. 'And when that comes we're finished.'

'My goodness, you people,' the Doctor said reproachfully. 'You do nothing but worry.'

Steven sighed and at that moment a high-pitched whining filled the chamber. 'What's that?'

'A signal that the ship is charged, unless I'm much mistaken.' He turned to the eye at the port. 'Is that so, my friend?'

'You are right, Doctor,' the Rill replied. 'We are ready to disconnect.'

The Doctor wanted to be sure as a Chumbley moved to disconnect the cable. 'You're sure you have enough power to lift off?'

'Sufficient to get us well into space where we can recharge from a sun.'

'Good, good. Well, that's it, we can go.'

'A machine will escort you back to your ship.'

'And you?' the Doctor asked.

'We will wait until you are safely there.'

'I'd rather you didn't. The moment I start my ship we're out of range in time. You need space. The moment we're clear, go.'

'Very well. The machine with you will escort you to your ship. It will protect you and obey your commands. Once you have gone it will destroy itself.'

Vicki was appalled: 'Oh, no.'

'It will be painless,' the Rill reassured her. 'It will simply put itself out of action, its job done. And now, we must bid you farewell. Our thanks again for your help.'

'And ours to you,' the Doctor said. 'Now get clear as fast as you can.'

'Goodbye, and take care.'

There was a click, and a humming noise filled the air. The chamber began to tremble. The Doctor led the way outside and he and his companions hastened to get clear, the Chumbley tweedling along beside them.

138

The hum became a mighty roaring. The Doctor and his party turned to watch the lift-off. A bright glow pulsated outward from the base of the Rills' ship, growing into such power that they could see the top of it vibrating against the menacingly ochrous sky.

Second followed second until they could see the ship literally straining to leap away, like a hound with all muscles gathered and waiting for the final spring. Then the restraining power was released, light and debris hurled themselves outward and the vessel leapt triumphantly up toward space. Momentarily it flickered before them, then was gone, the outbuildings now a mere heap of rubble to mark its passing. That take-off, the Doctor had to admit, was final proof of how advanced the Rills were – if proof were needed.

Maaga, too, had seen the departure and a bitter pill it was to swallow. Her hatred for the Rills would find no vent on them. But the Earth people still remained and now they no longer enjoyed the protection of their repulsive allies. She gestured to her two remaining soldiers and they set off toward the TARDIS, time snapping at their heels, out for the time-travellers' blood.

Now it struck. There was a powerful rumbling from underground and the very planet itself shook on its axis. The suns seemed to jump across the sky. The Doctor and his party raced onward, knowing that this was the end. The Chumbley suddenly stopped its perambulating about them, aimed its gun and fired, barely giving time for Maaga and her soldiers to take cover, which was the last delay they wanted because

139

their prey were now at the door of the TARDIS, the Doctor yanking out his key.

The soil split. Crevices raced across the surface and from them roared towering columns of molten lava. The air itself seemed to be tearing like paper. Suddenly the planet was a living hell, doomed to destruction, and taking all it could with it along the way.

As the Doctor and his friends fought their way breathlessly into the TARDIS Maaga turned to check on her soldiers, only to see them hurled upward atop a fresh jet of raging lava. She saw them only for a moment, racing upward like broken dolls, arms and legs akimbo, their hair wreaths of flame. Then they were gone.

Once inside the TARDIS the Doctor looked over to Steven and snapped, 'Quickly, the cable!'

Steven snatched it up and hurled it out into the blazing turmoil. He caught a fleeting glimpse of Maaga racing through the horror toward them and slammed the door shut. He leant gasping against it, and watched Vicki staring her sad last at the valiant Chumbley on the screen, which was still firing away at Maaga; and the Doctor, wrenching a lever over. The grinding sound of departure filled the console room and the Doctor blew out his cheeks with relief. It had been close.

Maaga stared in disbelief as the TARDIS demateri-alised. Deafened by the uproar, her clothes beginning to smoulder and her eyes stinging with acid tears, she turned upon the remaining Chumbley and blazed away at it. But it had shut down the moment the

TARDIS door had closed. Her ray sliced into it and it made no move. Its spirit had gone. She was alone.

White light raced across the surface. There was a deep bubbling sound, turning into one last bellow, and the planet exploded outward, debris hurling into outer space, and nothingness bursting in to delete existence for all time.

DOCTOR WHO

0426114558	**TERRANCE DICKS** **Doctor Who and The** **Abominable Snowmen**	£1.35
0426200373	**Doctor Who and The** **Android Invasion**	£1.25
0426201086	**Doctor Who and The** **Androids of Tara**	£1.35
0426116313	**IAN MARTER** **Doctor Who and The** **Ark in Space**	£1.35
0426201043	**TERRANCE DICKS** **Doctor Who and The** **Armageddon Factor**	£1.50
0426112954	**Doctor Who and The** **Auton Invasion**	£1.50
0426116747	**Doctor Who and The** **Brain of Morbius**	£1.35
0426110250	**Doctor Who and The** **Carnival of Monsters**	£1.35
042611471X	**MALCOLM HULKE** **Doctor Who and** **The Cave Monsters**	£1.50
0426117034	**TERRANCE DICKS** **Doctor Who and The** **Claws of Axos**	£1.35
042620123X	**DAVID FISHER** **Doctor Who and The** **Creature from the Pit**	£1.35
0426113160	**DAVID WHITAKER** **Doctor Who and The Crusaders**	£1.50
0426200616	**BRIAN HAYLES** **Doctor Who and The Curse** **of Peladon**	£1.50
0426114639	**GERRY DAVIS** **Doctor Who and The Cybermen**	£1.50
0426113322	**BARRY LETTS** **Doctor Who and The Daemons**	£1.50

Prices are subject to alteration

DOCTOR WHO

0426101103	DAVID WHITAKER **Doctor Who and The** **Daleks**	**£1.50**
042611244X	TERRANCE DICKS **Doctor Who and The Dalek** **Invasion of Earth**	**£1.50**
0426103807	**Doctor Who and The Day** **of the Daleks**	**£1.35**
042620042X	**Doctor Who – Death to** **the Daleks**	**£1.35**
0426119657	**Doctor Who and The** **Deadly Assassin**	**£1.50**
0426200969	**Doctor Who and The** **Destiny of the Daleks**	**£1.35**
0426108744	MALCOLM HULKE **Doctor Who and The** **Dinosaur Invasion**	**£1.35**
0426103726	**Doctor Who and** **The Doomsday Weapon**	**£1.50**
0426201464	IAN MARTER **Doctor Who and The** **Enemy of the World**	**£1.50**
0426200063	TERRANCE DICKS **Doctor Who and The** **Face of Evil**	**£1.50**
0426201507	ANDREW SMITH **Doctor Who – Full Circle**	**£1.50**
0426112601	TERRANCE DICKS **Doctor Who and The** **Genesis of the Daleks**	**£1.35**
0426112792	**Doctor Who and The Giant Robot**	**£1.35**
0426115430	MALCOLM HULKE **Doctor Who and The** **Green Death**	**£1.35**

Prices are subject to alteration

THIS OFFER EXCLUSIVE TO

DOCTOR WHO

READERS

Pin up magnificent full colour posters of DOCTOR WHO

Just send £2.50 for the first poster and £1.25 for each additional poster

TO: PUBLICITY DEPARTMENT *
    W. H. ALLEN & CO PLC
    44 HILL STREET
    LONDON W1X 8LB

Cheques, Postal Orders made payable to WH Allen PLC

POSTER 1 ☐   POSTER 2 ☐   POSTER 3 ☐
POSTER 4 ☐   POSTER 5 ☐

Please allow 28 DAYS for delivery.

I enclose £ _____

CHEQUE NO. _____

ACCESS, VISA CARD NO. _____

Name _____

Address _____

_____